OSLG

D1500321

# A SECRET
# UNTIL NOW

# A SECRET UNTIL NOW

BY

KIM LAWRENCE

MILLS & BOON®

First published in Great Britain 2014
by Mills & Boon, an imprint of Harlequin (UK) Limited,
Large Print edition 2014
Eton House, 18-24 Paradise Road,
Richmond, Surrey, TW9 1SR

© 2014 Kim Lawrence

ISBN: 978 0 263 24060 3

Harlequin (UK) Limited's policy is to use papers that
are natural, renewable and recyclable products and made
from wood grown in sustainable forests. The logging
and manufacturing processes conform to the legal
environmental regulations of the country of origin.

Printed and bound in Great Britain
by CPI Antony Rowe, Chippenham, Wiltshire

For my dad, Roy,
who was always proud of his writer daughter.

# PROLOGUE

*London, Summer 2008, a hotel*

ANGEL'S EYES HAD adjusted to the dark but from where she was lying the illuminated display of the bedside clock was hidden from her view, blocked by his shoulder. But the thin finger of light that was shining into the room through the chink in the blackout curtains suggested that it was morning.

'The morning after the night before!'

She gave a soft shaken sigh and allowed her glance to drift around the unfamiliar room, the generic but luxurious five-star hotel furnishings familiar, especially to someone who had slept in dozens of similar suites; someone who had imagined at one point that everybody ordered their supper from room service.

Since she'd had the choice Angel had avoided rooms like this as they depressed her. Depressed… Smiling at the past tense, she raised herself slowly up on one elbow. This room was different not because it boasted a special view or had a sumptuously comfortable bed. What was different was that she was not alone.

She froze when the man on the bed beside her murmured in his sleep and her attention immediately returned to him—it had never really left him. She gulped as he threw a hand above his head, the action causing the muscles in his beautiful back to ripple in a way that made her stomach flip over. She couldn't see his face but his breathing remained deep and regular.

Should she wake him up?

The bruised-looking half-moons underneath his spectacular eyes suggested he probably needed his sleep. She'd noticed them the moment she'd looked at him, but then she had noticed pretty much everything about him. Angel had never considered herself a particularly observant person but crazily one glance had indelibly printed his face into her memory.

Mind you, it was a pretty special face, not made any less special by the lines of fatigue etched around his wide, sensual mouth or the dark shadows beneath those totally spectacular eyes. There was a weary cynicism reflected in those electric-blue depths and also in that first instant anger.

He had been furious with her, but it wasn't the incandescent anger that had made her legs feel hollow or even her dramatic brush with death or that he had saved her life. It was him, everything about him. He projected an aura of raw male-ness that had a cataclysmic impact on her, like someone thrown in the deep end who from that first moment was treading water, barely able to breathe, throat tight with emotion as if she were submerged by a massive wave of lust.

It wasn't until much later that she had recognised this as a crossroad moment. She didn't see a fork in the road; there was no definable instant when she made a conscious decision. Her universe had narrowed into this total stranger, and she had known with utter and total conviction that she had to be with him. She wanted him and then she had seen in his eyes he wanted her too.

What else mattered?

*Did I really just think that?*

*What else mattered?* The defence of the greedy, absurdly needy and just plain stupid! Angel, who was utterly confident she was none of those things, was conscious that this particular inner dialogue was one it would have been more sensible to have had before, not *after*... After she had broken the habit of a lifetime and thrown caution, baby, bath water and the entire package out of the window!

The previous night there had been no inner dialogue, not even any inhibition-lowering alcohol in her bloodstream, no excuses. The words of a novel she had read years before popped into Angel's head. Although at the time they had made her put the gothic romance to one side with a snort of amused disdain, now she couldn't shake them. 'I felt a deep craving, an ache in my body and soul that I had never imagined possible.'

The remembered words no longer made her snigger and translate with a roll of her eyes— *yes, he's hot!*

Which the man in bed beside her was and then some, but Angel had met hot men before, and she had been amused by their macho posturing. She was in charge of her life and she liked it that way. History was littered with countless examples of strong women who had disastrous personal lives, but she was not going to be one of them.

Admittedly the macho men she was able to view with lofty disdain had not just saved her life, but Angel knew what she was feeling hadn't anything to do with gratitude. Beyond this certainty she wasn't sure of anything much. Her life and her belief system had been turned upside down. She had no idea at all why this was happening but she was not going to fight it. In any case, that would have been as futile as fighting the colour of her eyes or her blood type; it just was…and it was exciting!

'*Dio*, you're so beautiful.' Her husky whisper was soft and tinged with awe as she reached out a hand to touch his dark head, allowing her fingers to slide lightly over the sleek short tufts of hair. Her own hair was often called black but his was two shades darker and her skin, though a warm natural olive, looked almost winter pale against his deeply tanned, vibrant-toned, bronzed flesh. It was a contrast that had fascinated her when she'd first seen their limbs entwined—not just skin tone, but the tactile differences of his hard to her soft, his hair-roughened virility to her feminine smoothness. She wanted to touch, taste…

Angel couldn't understand how she felt so wide awake. Why she wasn't tired. She hadn't slept all night, but her senses weren't dulled by exhaustion. Instead they were racing and her body was humming with an almost painful sensory overload.

Languid pleasure twitched the corners of her full, wide mouth up as she lifted her arms above her head, stretching with feline grace, feeling muscles she hadn't known she had. Who wanted to sleep when it had finally happened? The man of her dreams was real and she had found him!

It was fate!

Her smooth brow knitted into a furrowed web. *Fate* again—this sounded so *not* her. When she had once been accused of not having a romantic bone in her body she had taken it as a compliment. She had never thought she was missing out; she'd never wanted to be that person—the one who fell in love at the drop of a hat and out again equally as easily. That was her mother who, despite the fragile appearance that made men want to protect her, had Teflon-coated emotions.

Angel knew she did not inspire a similar re-action in men and neither did she want to; the thought of not being independent was anathema to her. As a kid she had been saved from a life of loneliness and isolation by two things: a brother and an imagination. Not that she ever, even when she was young, confused her secret fantasy world with real life.

Angel had never expected her fantasies to ac-tually come true.

She stretched out her hand, moving her fingers in the air above the curve of his shoulder, fighting the compulsion to touch him, to tug the sheet that was lying low across his hips farther down. She was amazed that she could have these thoughts and feel no sense of embarrassment. It had been the same when she had undressed for him—it had just felt right and heart-stoppingly exciting.

No fantasy had ever matched the fascination she felt for his body. Her stomach muscles quiv-ered in hot, hungry anticipation of exploring every inch of his hard, lean body again.

'Totally beautiful,' she whispered again, star-ing at the man sharing her bed.

His name was Alex. When he'd asked she'd told

him her name was Angelina, but that nobody ever
called her that. Apparently when she was born
her father had said she looked like a little angel
and it had stuck.

She tensed when, as if in response to her voice,
he murmured in his sleep before rolling over onto
his back, one arm flung over his head, his long
fingers brushing the headboard.

Angel felt a strong sensual kick of excitement
low and deep in her belly as she stared, the rapt
expression on her face a fusion of awe and hunger. She swallowed past the emotional thickening that made her throat ache. He was the most
beautiful thing she had ever seen or imagined.

In the half-light that now filled the room his
warm olive-toned skin gleamed like gold, its
texture like oiled satin. A tactile tingle passed
through her fingertips. Perfect might have
seemed like an overused term but he was. The
length of his legs was balanced by broad shoulders and a deeply muscled chest dusted with dark
body hair that narrowed into a directional arrow
across his flat belly ridged with muscle. There
wasn't an ounce of excess flesh on his lean body
to disguise the musculature that had the perfec-

tion of an anatomical diagram. But Alex was no diagram. He was a warm, living, earthly male, and he was sharing her bed.

A dazed smile flickered across her face as she felt all the muscles in her abdomen tighten. Last night had been perfect—perfect, but not in the way she had expected. There had been hardly any pain and no embarrassment.

*Angel has still failed to grasp the concept of moderation. There is no middle ground—she is all or nothing.*

The words on her report card came back to her.

Her form teacher had been referring to her academic record littered with As and Fs, not to sex, but there had been no middle ground last night either. Angel had held nothing back; she had given him everything without reservation.

'I know this is bad timing, but there's a problem.'

The words had been music to Alex's ears. 'Tell me.'

They had and he had acted. Crisis management was something he excelled at—it was a simple matter of focusing, shutting out all distractions and focusing.

He had gone straight from the funeral to his office, where he'd pretty much lived for the past month. He'd washed, eaten and slept—or at least snatched a few minutes on the sofa—there. It made sense, and it suited him. He had nothing to go home to any longer.

Then the crisis was over and Alex had been unable to think of any reason not to go home, where he had, if anything, less sleep. He did go to bed but by the small hours he was up again, which was why it felt strange and disorientating to wake up after a deep sleep and find light shining through the blinds of...not his room... Where the hell?

He blinked and focused on the beautiful face of the most incredible-looking woman. She was sitting there looking down at him wearing nothing but a mane of glossy dark hair that lay like a silky curtain over her breasts—breasts that had filled his hands perfectly and tasted—

It all came rushing back.

Hell!

'Good morning.'

His body reacted to the slumberous promise in her smile, but, ignoring the urgent messages it was sending and the desire that heated his blood, gritted his teeth and swung his legs over the side of the bed. Guilt rising like a toxic tide to clog his throat, he sat, eyes closed, with his rigid back to her. This was about damage limitation and not repeating a mistake no matter how tempting it might seem.

She was sinful temptation given a throaty voice and a perfect body, but this had been his mistake, not hers, and it was his responsibility to end it.

'I thought you'd never wake up.'

His spine tensed at the touch of her fingers on his skin. He wiped his face of all emotion as he turned back to face her.

'You should have woken me. I hope I haven't made you late for anything…?'

'Late…?' she quavered.

He stood up and looked around for his clothes. 'Can I get you a taxi?'

'I…I don't understand… I thought we'd…' Her voice trailed away. He was looking at her so coldly.

'Look, last night was… Actually it was fantastic but I'm not available.'

*Available?* Angel still didn't get it.

He felt the guilt tighten in his gut but he had no desire to prolong this scene. He'd made a massive mistake, end of story. A post-mortem was not going to change anything.

'I thought—'

He cut across her. 'Last night was just sex.'

He was speaking slowly as if he were explaining something to a child or a moron. The coldness in his blue eyes as much as his words confused Angel.

'But last night...'

'Like I said, last night was great, but it was a mistake.' A great big mistake, but a man learned by his mistakes and he didn't give in to the temptation to repeat them.

She began to feel sick as she watched him fight his way into his shirt, then he was pulling on his trousers. She responded automatically to pick up the object that fell out of the pocket and landed with a metallic twang on the floor just in front of her toes. She bent to pick it up; her fingers closed around a ring.

'*Yours?*'

He was meticulously careful not to touch her fingers as he took it from her outstretched hand.

'You're married?'

For a moment he thought of telling the truth, saying that he had been, but no longer, that the ring was in his pocket because friends kept telling him it was time to move on. Alex doubted this was what they'd had in mind.

Then he realised how much easier and less painful a lie would be. It wouldn't ease the guilt that was like a living thing in his gut, but it would make this scene less messy and allow her to say when regaling her friends later that *the bastard was married.*

'I'm sorry.'

Her incredible green eyes flared hot as she rose majestically to her feet and delivered a contemptuous 'You disgusting loser!' followed up by a backhanded slap that made him blink. He opened his watering eyes in time to see her vanish into the bathroom, the door locked audibly behind her.

Angel ran, hand clamped to her mouth, across the room, just making it to the loo before she was violently sick.

By the time she returned to the bedroom he was gone.

Angel found herself hating him with more

venom than she thought she was capable of. She
hated him even more than her mother's creepy
boyfriend, the one who had tried to grope her
when she was sixteen. The only person she hated
more than Alex was herself. How could she be so
stupid? He had treated her like a tramp because
that was how she had acted.

By the time she left the hotel room later that
morning, her tears had dried and her expression
was set. She had decided she would never, ever
think of him again, not think of him or last night.

It never happened.

He never existed.

It was a solution.

She could move on.

# CHAPTER ONE

'THEY ARE THE second biggest advertising firm in Europe and—'

'There is something in it for you?' Alex, who had been listening to Nico's pitch while he read the small print on a contract, made the silky suggestion without rancour. He liked his big sister's son and why should his favourite, actually his only, nephew be any different from everyone else?

The younger man acknowledged the point with a self-conscious shrug. 'Well, I had heard there might be an internship going…?'

Alex finished reading, wrote his signature on the last page of the document and laid it on top of the done pile before pushing his chair back and stretching his long legs out in front of him. He flexed his shoulders and thought wistfully about the run he had promised himself as a reward for spending the morning at his desk. Not that he begrudged the youngster his time—Nico was a low-maintenance relative, unlike some who looked on him as their own personal bank. He was philosophical about the role but family was important.

'Consider the decks cleared. You have my attention.'

'Good of you.' But not entirely comfortable for him as his uncle Alex's eyes had always reminded Nico of ice chips. It wasn't the colour, although that was an unnerving pale blue, as his own mother shared the same strangely coloured eyes with her much younger brother. It was the impression he'd had as a kid that those eyes had always been able to see right into his head. He was no longer a kid but he was always painfully honest around his uncle—just in case.

'You know that Dad's offered me a job and I'm grateful,' came the hasty assurance.

Alex voiced the unspoken addendum. 'But?'

'But I'd like to do something that didn't have anything to do with being his son or your nephew.'

'I admire your intentions if not your practicality, and you seem to forget I was born with a silver spoon.'

'And you turned it gold,' the young man said gloomily.

There was no firm on the brink of the financial abyss for Nico to save. Thanks to Alex the shipping empire founded by his Greek great grandfather had recovered from years of mismanagement and had gone from strength to strength to be hailed as one of the success stories of the global recession.

Of course even if it hadn't his uncle would still be fabulously rich as Alex had inherited the Arlov vast oil fortune a few years earlier from the Russian great grandfather that Nico had never met. That was when Alex had delegated the day-to-day running of the shipping business to his brother-in-law, Nico's father.

'And that is a bad thing?'

'No, of course not, but no one thinks of you as a little rich boy who's never done a day's work in his life.'

A direct quote? Alex wondered, feeling a stab of sympathy for his nephew, who was all of the above but also a rather nice kid.

'You don't have anything to prove.' His eyes fell. 'Just forget it,' he mumbled. 'I knew I was talking out of my… I guess I knew you wouldn't be up for it. I just wanted to impress the guy from the advertising firm and you should have seen his face when I mentioned your island, Saronia. He lit up like a firework. Pathetic or what.' He reached out for the tablet he had opened on his uncle's desk and drew back as Alex withdrew it from his reach.

'You were trying to impress. Why apologise? Unless your interest is more personal? I am assuming the new *face* of this cosmetic firm is not ugly—one of your actress friends perhaps? Are you still dating…?' The name of the pretty girl from the soap escaped him as he idly scrolled down the screen that showed the logo of the cosmetics giant that was apparently launching a new perfume.

It was not a world that Alex knew much about. 'A big thing, is it, a new perfume?'

'Massive,' his nephew assured him. 'They're planning to make a series of ads to promote it using the same couple, six ads in all, really glossy and high production values, like a kind of serial each with a story and a cliffhanger like a romantic minisoap. They've got a big-name director and this guy from Hollywood to star in it—though he must be at least thirty-five.'

Alex fought a smile. 'That old!' Good to know he had three years to go before he was classed as elderly by his nephew.

'They want to film the first three in an exotic setting—sand, sun and palm trees on an island paradise thing.'

'And a connection with the golden age of Hollywood would not hurt,' Alex inserted. He could see why Saronia would appeal to them as a location.

In its day the island had been the setting for his grandfather's famous parties. Spyros Theakis—a man with a well-documented taste for starlets—reaping the financial rewards of his successful Greek shipping empire, had hosted lavish parties attended by all the stars of the day on his private island. The photos of those legendary events still surfaced from time to time, as did the tales of wild parties, torrid affairs and general excess. Most left out the fact that the mansion had been burnt down during an electrical storm. By some miracle none of the guests had been seriously hurt but the place had never been rebuilt. His grandfather's fortunes, like those of the island, had gone into decline and the place had become uninhabited.

Alex had visited out of curiosity when the resort hotel he had commissioned was being built on the mainland just a few minutes away by boat. Emma, who had come with him, had been fascinated by the romance of the place. They had always planned to build a house there but the plans had been put on hold when she'd become ill and had been shelved permanently after the diagnosis.

He had gone back to Saronia for the first time a few months after her death, camping on the beach for a few days that had stretched into several weeks. Later that year he had commissioned a house, not the family house that he had planned with Emma but a small place, minimalist, no frills—though not the monk's cell his sister had called it. It was his own retreat; he went there once or twice a year to recharge his batteries.... God knew there were few places where he could guarantee there were no photographers lurking around the corner, no phones, no news—he was off the grid when he was there.

As much as he admired his nephew's enterprise he would sooner have invited cameras into his own bathroom than allow a film crew to invade this precious private sanctuary.

'Louise,' the younger man said suddenly as he took a seat on the edge of the big desk. 'She had a really tough upbringing and she thinks I'm... spoilt.'

'This is your soap star?'

Nico nodded.

'And you want to impress her.' Alex, who had been idly scrolling through the tablet, stopped. 'Who is that?' The lack of inflection in his voice might have made those who knew him better wonder...but Nico's attention was on his own troubled love life, not the sudden tension in his uncle's body language.

His nephew bent over, scanning the inverted image that filled the screen. It was a studio shot of an extremely beautiful young woman pouting provocatively at the camera with lips that were glossy and scarlet. Everything about her was provocative, from the swathe of dark wavy hair that fell artistically across one half of her face to the smile in her heavily lidded eyes, a smile that seemed to invite you to share a secret that gleamed in the shimmering emerald depths as she leaned forward displaying a large amount of cleavage in a gold sheath dress that clung like a second skin.

'Angel. She's a model.'

Angel... Angelina? 'A model.'

It did not surprise him. What did surprise him was the instant effect of a face he had last seen six years ago.... An incident that had not been his finest hour, but one he had consigned to the past. The instant surge of sexual hunger that tightened in his belly had a very *present* feel to it.

His nephew nodded and looked amazed by his uncle's ignorance. 'You must have seen her in that underwear campaign last year. She was everywhere.'

'I must have missed that one,' he mused, seeing the beautiful sleek brunette not in underwear... not in anything. He went to stand but, not wanting to draw attention to the testosterone that had suddenly pooled in his groin, he sat back down again like some hormonal teenager, resenting his lack of control—or at least the cause of it.

'Gorgeous, isn't she?' the young man continued, oblivious to any undercurrents in the air. 'All that hair and those green eyes. They are going to build the campaign around her. It's a calculated risk, they said, not to choose a big celebrity to be the new face for a perfume, but they want to build the campaign around someone who—'

Alex tuned out the explanation of the thinking behind employing a relative unknown—she was not unknown to him. Seeing that face, those eyes, remembering the sleek, sinuous body, the undulating curves, the golden toned skin, brought that night back so clearly that he could smell the scent of her shampoo.

Lust slammed through him again like an iron fist. With it came the guilt…always the guilt. Emma dead how many weeks…? And he had jumped into bed with the first available woman. She had led but he had followed.

His lips curled in self-disgust. He had moved on since then, when he'd felt ready. Not one-night stands, that was not his thing, but he had enjoyed a series of satisfying relationships with women who enjoyed sex but not drama, and none had been tainted with guilt. If that required he maintain a certain emotional distance it was a price worth paying.

'Yes.'

He had no desire to revisit that place of agonising guilt but to recapture that…? It was not so much a *thing* he was trying to recapture but an absence that he was trying to fill. He gave his head a tiny shake, aware that he was guilty of the sin of overanalysing. She had been the best sex of his life, so why not make a push to sample it and her again?

Nico, who had taken his ringing mobile phone from his pocket intending to turn it off, dropped it. It lay where it had fallen as, jaw slack with shock, he scanned the face of the man who sat behind the big desk, a pointless exercise because he never could read his uncle.

'Whaddaya… Yes…?' he said, unable to believe he was this lucky.

Behind the desk Alex brought his formidable mental control into play and pushed the increasingly erotic images from his head.

He raised one dark brow. 'Yes.'

Nico surged to his feet, radiating the sort of youthful excitement that made Alex, who was all of what, twelve years his senior, feel old. 'Seriously…? This isn't a wind-up… No, you don't—'

Alex quirked a dark brow and suggested, 'Have a sense of humour?'

Maybe the boy was right; maybe he had eradicated that along with his conscience.

A conscience was an inconvenient thing, he thought, seeing the expression in those big eyes. He needed to draw a line under what had happened, and this was an unexpected opportunity to do just that. A girl who adopted a 'jump into bed first and ask questions later' policy should have expected a few surprises, yet innocence was an odd word to use with someone who had been so sexually uninhibited. But for some reason…? Again, he was overthinking this.

Take away the acrid taste of guilt and she remained the best sex he had ever had, and due to pressures of work it had been months since he had enjoyed any sex, which might go some way to explaining the strength of his physical response. He didn't try to justify it. He didn't just need sex, he needed a question mark in his life;

he needed highs and lows, not a predictable flat-line monotony.

Wondering where that thought had come from, he was aware he sounded like a man who was not satisfied with his life. He was; of course he was. Alex got to his feet and picked up the jacket he had slung over the back of the chair.

'You going to pick that up?' He nodded towards the phone.

Looking dazed, his nephew nodded. 'What...? Oh, sure...'

'You will keep me up to speed?'

'Me? You want me to... Great, of course... So should I run the details past...?' Though tall and blessed with an athletic build, the younger man was forced to tilt his head back to look up at his uncle who, at six-five, was a couple of inches taller than him, and significantly more than a couple inches broader across the shoulders.

'Me,' Alex said, shrugging on a fine wool jacket that was tailored to fit across his broad shoulders so it fell into place without a crease.

'You really mean this? You'll actually let them film on Saronia?'

He'd made the pitch but in his wildest dreams

Nico had never seriously expected it to work. Everyone knew how jealously Alex Arlov protected his privacy, even more so since someone had hacked into his wife's medical records not long before she died. It was after the resulting tearjerking newspaper article that he had gained the reputation of being ferociously litigious, someone prepared to go after perpetrators who crossed the line in the sand regardless of the cost. Some people suggested that this meant he had something to hide, and pointed out the lives he had ruined by taking legal retribution, but they did so in very small voices and only after taking extensive legal advice!

Nico, who was not averse to seeing his own picture on the pages of celebrity magazines, privately considered that Uncle Alex took it a bit far. The paparazzo who had ended up fully clothed in a swimming pool at his mother's birthday bash last year, camera and all, might have agreed with him.

'With certain restrictions obviously. They stay on the mainland and make the daily commute. I don't want them anywhere near the house. I can leave the details with you?'

'Wow... Yes, absolutely and, thanks, you won't regret this.'

Alex watched the boy bounce from the room oozing enthusiasm and incredulous joy. If Alex had been the type to dwell on the motivations behind his decision he might have spent the next hour doing so with increasing frustration. But he wasn't, so he spent the next hour running instead.

Angel poked her head around the door of the lounge where most of the people involved had congregated. Used to the handful involved in a fashion shoot, she thought there seemed to be an awful lot of them.

'I think I'll go for a walk. Anyone fancy some fresh air?' She was an active person, and being cooped up in the claustrophobic atmosphere of the luxury hotel was getting to her.

Several astonished pairs of eyes turned her way. Someone whose name she had forgotten replied, his tone indulgent, 'It's raining, Angel, honey.'

*It never rains in August.*

Angel had lost count of the number of times she had heard this statement since they had arrived at the resort, but the fact remained that, despite the lack of precedent, it was raining and it had been for two days solid. In fact, it had been ever since they had arrived at the island paradise, this paradise they had yet to set foot on.

The delay to the photo shoot had caused tempers to fray and the money men to start muttering. For Angel it was two days she could have been at home with her daughter, not hundreds of miles away.

'It's just water.'

Her response drew blank looks. 'But you'll get wet.'

'I need the exercise.'

'I'm just off to the gym,' said India, the actress playing her mother in the ad—though the woman was only ten years older than Angel. 'Come with me.'

'I don't really do the gym thing. I'm allergic to Lycra.'

'Seriously?'

'No, not seriously, India, she's joking,' Rudie, the lighting man, explained.

'Your hair will get wet.' The objection was made by the man responsible for making her hair look perfect. He was still recovering from the shock of discovering that, not only was the waist-length ebony hair all her own, but the glossy colour had never been enhanced or altered.

'It will dry.'

'What's that smell?'

'Me, I'm afraid.' Angel brought her concealed hand out from behind her back. 'I can't resist lashings of onions.'

'Is that a hot dog?'

Angel glanced at the item that was causing the executive from the cosmetic company to look so shocked. The only person in the room who didn't seem horrified was the handsome young Greek, Nico. She assumed from his appearance he was one of the Theakis family who owned the luxury resort and any number of others around the world, and probably the shipping line of the same name, but she wasn't sure what his connection was with the owner of Saronia who he was representing.

'I really hope so.'

Again the young Greek was the only one to laugh so she winked at him and murmured, 'Tough crowd to play,' in a terrible New York drawl.

'But you had a full breakfast.' The critical follow-up came from the stylist.

Walking in the rain had clearly not been received well, but she could tell from the general air of disapproval in the room that eating an actual meal was considered aberrant behaviour by those present. But Angel coped with their disapproval by refusing to recognise it.

The same way she had refused to recognise the broad hints earlier that she might be better selecting a pot of low-fat yogurt rather than a full English. She was all for a peaceful life.

'And it was delicious.' Angel could feel the woman staring at her as though they expected to see her developing unsightly bulges as she watched.

Her grip on her hot dog tightened as she fought the urge to say something that would make everyone look at her with the opposite of their current disdain. It had taken time, but she had conquered her need to seek approval, recognising late in the day that the one person—her mother—from whom she wanted that approval was never going to give it.

Only very occasionally these days did she find

that eager-to-please tendency resurfacing. When it did she quashed it ruthlessly. Needy was just not a good look, and not the sort of example she wanted to set for her daughter.

She lifted her chin and embraced them all with a brilliant smile. 'Then it's just as well I'm going to go for a walk.'

The figure who had been hiding behind a newspaper lowered it, revealing the lived-in features of a photographer who was more famous than the A-list people who posed for him.

'Relax, guys, our girl here never puts on an ounce. Do you, darling?' His brows lifted as his glance slid down the supple curves of the young woman framed in the doorway. 'Looking particularly lush this morning.... Purely a professional observation, you understand, Angel, luv.'

Alex nodded to a gardener whose eyes widened as he recognised the person who had manoeuvred his way past the ladder he had set up against the trellis.

Alex liked to fly under the radar when he could. He had arrived the previous night in a private jet that had landed at a private airport and had made the short crossing alone in the rain that had been falling ever since. It was, according to the information supplied by his spy in the camp, Nico, playing havoc with the filming schedule.

The rain had just stopped and the dampness underfoot was already being turned to misty vapour by the late-afternoon sun. Someone had forgotten to adjust the sprinkler system, which was adding to the moisture, but a few of the holidaymakers had already begun to venture out of the hotel, including a large family group who were playing a boisterous game of cricket on the beach.

Alex had a few hours to kill before the meet-and-greet cocktail party Nico had arranged later that evening. The young man thought that Alex was making the effort to attend as a favour to him. Alex, whose motivation was far less selfless, had seen no harm in letting his young relative—and by association his older sister—think just that. It was always handy to have a favour in hand with his sibling.

Heading towards the noise on the beach, he made his way down the flower-filled terraces that led to the tree-lined walkway above the beach. Normally at this time of day it would have been dotted with parasols and supine brown bodies, but the weather meant it was almost empty except for the family group in the midst of their raucous ball game.

Alex was conscious of an uncharacteristic impatience as he anticipated the evening ahead. The tall, luscious brunette had been the best sex of his life, and he had felt nothing that had approached that level of carnal passion since. But would the incredible chemistry between them still be there?

Seeing her face had definitely aroused the dormant hunting instincts in him, and, though Alex had no intention of investing emotionally in any relationship, he had normal appetites.

He shook his head and decided he would spend the remainder of the evening running through the details of the extension project with the contractors that would double the size of the spa. He was a firm believer in multitasking; to combine business with pleasure was a pragmatism he was comfortable with, but he was considerably less comfortable with the inescapable scent of obsession attached to moving heaven and earth to engineer a meeting with a one-night stand from six years ago.

Thinking it over did not remove her face from his head. Instead, it was the ball that was hurtling towards him at great speed that did that. It would have hit him had not some sixth sense made him turn his head and, without thinking, he shot out his hand to catch it.

There was a ripple of applause to congratulate this display of lightning reflexes and natural coordination, followed by a chorus of apologies from the beach. He nodded acknowledgment and responded to the light-hearted invitation to join in the fun from the players with a negative motion of his head before he tossed the ball back and continued along the wide boulevard.

'Go deep, go deep!'

Someone was yelling, and he turned his head and saw a figure who was doing her level best to follow the instruction. It was a figure who… He stopped dead. Alex had imagined the object of his lustful machinations sunning herself, maybe topless? Sipping a cocktail or taking advantage of the spa facilities, but not pelting across the sand barefoot in a pair of shorts and a cut-off T-shirt, her hair flying and yelling wildly.

'I've got it!'

Before he had a chance to assimilate this extraordinary turn of events she caught the ball, released an exultant whoop, jumped high in the air and was promptly wrestled to the ground by one of the male players. Alex watched with distaste as they rolled around on the ground, the man's hands seemingly everywhere. It was one of those moments when a man felt the layers of civilisation peel away, and he wasn't aware until he had begun to walk rapidly away that his hands were clenched into fists.

Angel, hot, sweaty and deeply involved in the match, didn't see the throw but she did see the distant figure fling the ball back with an accuracy that caused a second ripple of applause.

There were millions of tall, dark, athletically built, handsome men in the world and some of them projected an aura of authority and, well... sex. So over the years she had experienced a few heart-thudding, stomach-clenching moments of shocked recognition only to discover after all the breathless anticipation that as the object of her antipathy got nearer it was not HIM, but a pale imitation who did not possess that level of raw sensuality that she had responded to on a primal level.

But she was a mother now and her primal days were in the past. The chances she would ever meet HIM—she always thought of Jas's father in capital letters—again were remote, and if she ever did it was not likely it would be here, she thought, tearing her eyes from the tall figure. Even though she knew it wasn't HIM, her heart was still racing as she followed the bellowed instruction to go deep from the bowler, a ten-year-old who had a well-developed competitive streak.

When she did catch the ball a few moments later she found herself rugby tackled by the handsome husband of the woman who had invited her to join the game. When she disentangled herself and emerged triumphantly holding the ball aloft the suited figure on the broad walkway who had dredged up memories that were better left undisturbed was gone.

# CHAPTER TWO

AT THE END of an exhausting game the friendly family invited her to take afternoon tea with them as they were celebrating the grandparents' diamond anniversary. Refusal, they told her, was not an option, so after nipping back to her bungalow to quickly shower and change she joined them in a private lounge where she ate cakes and no one pointed out the fat content.

It was the first time Angel had enjoyed herself since she had arrived, or even come close to relaxing, though watching one of the grandchildren who was Jasmine's age did make her throat swell with emotion as she wondered what her daughter was doing.

As a result, she ate more cake and stayed longer than she'd intended. So after the lively afternoon the silence and emptiness of her bungalow felt rather depressing. Not that it wasn't a lovely room—actually it was a two-bedroom suite furnished in a very expensive version of rustic, with dark, chunky wooden furniture and floors with splashes of colour provided by the original art displayed on the white walls.

All the bungalows had flower-bedecked private terraces with spa tubs, some with a view of the pool with its mountain backdrop; others, like the one that Angel had been allocated, had a sea view. The sand lapped by the turquoise waves was sugary white and dotted with palms. The storm of the previous day seemed a dim and distant memory this evening.

Before stepping back into her room Angel dusted the sand off the soles of her bare feet. It was not hard to see why the place was popular with honeymooning couples lucky enough to be able to afford the prices the very upmarket resort charged. But then paradise didn't come cheap. As gorgeous as it was, the place lacked a vital ingredient that was essential for Angel's paradise.

God, she thought, giving her head a tiny shake before she crossed the room to the side table, her bare feet silent on the wooden floor. Her chest tightened and she felt the sting of tears in her eyes as she picked up the framed photo of Jasmine.

'Here five minutes and homesick already! Your mum is a wimp,' she told the picture of the laughing child before she kissed the glass, swallowed the emotional lump in her throat and with a brisk, 'Pull yourself together, Angel,' she replaced it carefully on the side table.

Then after a last wave to the photo she straightened her shoulders and headed for the open French doors, pausing to slip her feet into a pair of flat sandals as she headed for the bedroom. It had been made very clear that the drinks party was not optional! And she was… She glanced at her wristwatch. Yes, she was running late.

So no time to change.

'Drinks and butter up the rich owner…?' She pursed her lips, staring as she aimed a frown at her reflection in the full-length mirror.

The frown was for the rich owner who would most likely have a monumental ego, and the question was purely rhetorical. The thin cotton dress she was wearing was not by any stretch a cocktail dress. It was little more than an ankle-length cover-up she had chosen earlier, a deep cobalt blue shot with swirls of green. It left her smooth brown shoulders bare, or they would have been if it hadn't been for the straps of her halter bikini.

Angel might move in the world of high fashion but she was no slave to the latest trends. She knew what suited her; she had an individual style and the confidence to carry off anything she wore.

Poise, the scout from the talent agency had called it. It was, he had told her later, the reason he had picked her out from countless pretty girls in the park that day, that and the length of her legs. Her legs *were* quite good, and Angel and the scout were quite good friends these days despite the fact that her brother, witnessing the first encounter, had warned the middle-aged man off in no uncertain terms. Her brother was the only male of her acquaintance who thought her incapable of taking care of herself. Exasperating, but she tolerated it because she knew his intentions were good, though his methods sometimes a bit Neanderthal.

She reached the bow behind her neck and, tongue caught between her teeth, managed to unclip the fastener of her bikini. She gave a grunt as she managed to whip it off without disturbing the dress. Already moving towards the door, she slung the top on the bed as she twitched the neckline, pulling it a few modest centimetres higher over the slopes of her breasts as she glanced in the mirror.

'Or should we add the pearls?' She chuckled to herself before warning her mirror image darkly, 'First signs of madness, Angel.' Snatching up the string of pretty green beads she'd bought at a crazy cheap price from an enterprising trader before a security guard had given him marching orders from the private stretch of beach, she left the bungalow at a trot, looping them around her neck as she went, reflecting it wasn't what you wore, it was the way you wore it. A cliché but true nonetheless.

It was rare that Alex felt the need to rationalise his own actions, and why should he now? Looking at the situation objectively, all he had done was agree to Nico's request. He'd helped out his nephew, which was what families did. Plus, he had business here. It was called multitasking, he told himself.

He was curious, no crime. It wasn't as if he had

engineered the situation solely for the purpose of meeting with the woman who had spent the night in his bed six years ago.

*Sure you didn't, Alex—you were just passing.*

Of course, if he took advantage of a situation that had fallen into his lap, who could blame him?

The last time she had not fallen in his lap, she had jumped!

Alex, who believed contrary to popular belief very few people were capable of learning from past mistakes, was an advocate of living in the present. But as a pulse of hot lust slammed through his body he found his thoughts being dragged back to a moment six years ago, when, driven by the need he'd had then to fill his every waking moment with action, he had left his car and driver stuck in rush-hour traffic and walked instead along a crowded London street.

If he hadn't been...?

She had stepped off the pavement into the moving traffic and he had literally dragged the young woman from underneath the wheels of a bus.

The memory, a moment frozen in time etched on his brain, was so vivid he could smell the exhaust fumes in the air now, hear the tortured squeal of brakes and the cry of a solitary onlooker who, alone among those busily going about their own business, had witnessed the moment of near disaster.

Alex's reaction had been pure reflex, not related in any way to bravery, and his body's response had been equally involuntary when he'd turned the figure around and looked down into the face turned up to him...and carried on looking.

His anger had melted.

She was stunning!

He could remember thinking what a crime it would have been for that face to be marked. A delicate, slightly tip-tilted nose; wide, full, luscious lips; a natural pout even in repose and incredible deep green, heavily lashed, almond-shaped eyes set beneath thick, darkly defined, arched brows, and all that general gorgeousness set against flawless satiny skin that had glowed pale gold in the grey city street.

He'd found himself holding the breathing embodiment of sensuality and his body had responded accordingly and instantaneously.

Fighting the impulse to keep her plastered

against his body for longer—there was no way she couldn't have picked up on how hard he was—he'd released her, but retained a steadying hold of her elbows as he'd pushed her a little away. His nostrils had flared as the scent of her shampoo had drifted his way.

She had been breathing hard and blinking in a dazed way. Even in the flat, unattractive boots she'd been wearing she'd been tall for a woman, reaching a little past his shoulder. Her slim but voluptuous curves had made the generic jeans and T-shirt she wore look anything but common.

'Are you all right?'

She'd nodded, sending the magnificent waist-length curtain of hair that shone like polished ebony silk swishing around her face. He'd watched as, head tilted forward, she did a sweep of her feet upwards.

'It's all still there and in one piece,' she'd murmured, sounding dazed. Her voice had had a delicious throaty rasp. 'You really do see your life pass before your eyes.' She'd tilted her head back and looked at him, breathing a soft 'Wow!' as her eyes widened.

He had found himself grinning, amused by her

total lack of artifice, then watched in fascination as a visible wave of heat travelled up the long graceful curve of her neck, adding an extra tinge of colour to her smooth cheeks. He could not remember ever encountering a woman who wore her emotions so close to the surface. Yet despite the blush, the glowing, gorgeous young creature had held his gaze steadily.

'I think you saved my life.'

He'd given the faintest of shrugs. 'Do you make a habit of throwing yourself under moving vehicles?'

She'd then been staring as hard at him as he was at her. 'It was a first for me.'

When not breathless, the throaty, sexy quality of her voice had intensified.

He'd felt her trembling. Post-trauma or was she feeling the same clutch of lust he was…?

There'd been more than a hint of provocative challenge in her attitude as she'd lifted her chin and asked, 'Can I… Let me buy you a coffee, to thank you…? It seems the least I can do, unless you're…?'

'Coffee would be good,' he'd heard himself say.

She had expelled a tiny sigh and beamed up at

him in undisguised delight, and when he'd kept a guiding hand on one of her elbows she hadn't pulled away. He'd felt her shiver and that time he'd known why.

Alex pushed away the memory; as always it was inextricably and painfully linked in his mind with guilt. On one level he recognised the guilt was irrational. He had no longer been married at that point, hadn't cheated, he'd been free to have sex with a total stranger.

Even when Emma had been alive he could have taken a mistress with her blessing. Alex was not easily shocked but on the first occasion she had brought the subject up he had been—deeply. He'd known she'd had something on her mind and had coaxed her to tell him what was bothering her but he hadn't been prepared for the incendiary suggestion she had made.

'You're a man, you have needs that I can't…and you've been so patient with me, never said that I should have told you about the MS. I wanted to, but it might have been years before it came back or even never.'

'It wouldn't have made any difference if I had

known,' he had told her, hoping it was true. Even wondering had felt like a betrayal.

'I know that, Alex, but the fact remains you didn't have the choice. I didn't give you the choice. So if you need to, you know...date other women, that's all right with me. I don't have to know, I don't want to know, so long as you stay with me while I'm— I hate hospitals so much, Alex...'

And there it was, the real fear, that he would send her to some anonymous nursing home. It had cut him to the core to know his wife had been willing to endure infidelities for the security and promise of staying in the home that she had enjoyed furnishing in those first months of marriage. She had enjoyed a lot of things before the disease that had finally killed her resurfaced.

A short year later she had been confined to a wheelchair and eaten up with guilt because she hadn't told him before they'd got married. The constant apologising had been hard to hear and sometimes had made him angry with her. Guilt piled on top of more guilt. It had been a vicious circle.

'This is your home, Emma, our home.' Her

hand had felt so small under his, the bones fragile as he'd squeezed. 'There will be no hospitals and no other women, I swear.'

And he had kept his word to the letter if not the spirit. He might have been legally free but in his mind, in his heart, Alex had still been married when he had spent the night with Angelina. Though not once during that night had he thought of Emma. How could he have forgotten, even for a moment? The next morning he hadn't been able to get out of there quickly enough.

If he had encountered the stunning Angel when Emma had still been alive would he have found it so easy to keep his promise? The question wouldn't go away and he would never know the answer, but he was pretty sure that if he had it wouldn't have given him any comfort.

Alex liked to think he was able to forgive weakness in others, but he set higher standards for himself. Though he'd got out of there as fast as he could the morning after, memories of the night before had haunted him. Well, he was about to lay that ghost—literally if things turned out as he intended—to rest.

'Only the star is missing.' His inability to prevent his eyes going to the doorway sent a surge of irritation through Alex. 'Does the lady like to make an entrance?'

Beside him Nico responded defensively to the disdain in his uncle's voice. 'She's really nice.'

The balding executive whom he had directed his sardonic comment to nodded in agreement with his nephew's assessment. 'She certainly doesn't stand on ceremony and the last thing you can accuse her of is being a diva.' He laughed at some private joke and took a sip of the orange juice he was nursing. 'And if she wanted people to notice her she wouldn't need any stunts. With Angel in the room no one else exists.' He drew a line in the air and pronounced with utter confidence, 'End of story.'

Alex recalled Angelina, or Angel as it seemed he must learn to call her, in his room, an anonymous hotel room. For him that night, no one else had existed. He clenched his teeth in an effort to eject the image of her sitting on the bed gloriously naked and utterly unselfconscious, acting as if they had just shared more than lust, acting as if there would be a tomorrow.

Dragging himself into the present, he wondered

if the executive's admiration was purely professional. Was the man sleeping with the model? He
knew little of the world they occupied but he supposed it would hardly be a revelation if they were.

'Rudie says Angel simply doesn't have a bad
angle. The camera loves her,' Nico, the new pres-
ident of her fan club, informed him.

'And Rudie is?'

'Our lighting man, one of the best.'

The guy was probably in love with her too,
Alex thought sourly.

Oh, God, she was the last to arrive. Angel fought
the impulse to step back into the shadows, then
smiled to herself at the irony that she made her
living posing for a camera, having her image
stared at by the public, though she genuinely
hated being the centre of attention.

She didn't retreat but paused in the doorway,
her eyes sweeping the room, the light breeze pulling the silky fluttering fabric of her dress against
long legs until Ross spotted her. The photographer grinned, giving a thumbs-up sign, in the
process slopping what she knew would be tonic
water down his front. People assumed he had a

drink problem, and he let them think that. He had once confided to Angel that he simply didn't like the taste of alcohol, but being thought an ex-alcoholic made him seem more interesting.

Angel's spontaneous burst of throaty laughter alerted the others to her presence and she was immediately involved in a lot of luvvie air kissing.

Well, she'd been right about one thing: she was underdressed. The men, with the exception of Ross, were wearing suits and ties and the women cocktail dresses.

'Worth the wait,' he heard someone say and Alex could not disagree.

The late arrival's appearance had sent a rush of scalding heat through his body. Six years ago she had been stunning, possessing a natural grace and sleek sensuality that had been all the more powerful for appearing totally unstudied. She still possessed all those attributes but now she held herself with the confidence that came when a woman knew the power she wielded with her beauty, when she enjoyed it.

Every man in the room was enjoying it.

Alex's enjoyment was tempered by this knowledge and the discomfort that could be traced to the testosterone-fuelled ache in his groin. The intervening years slipped away as his blue eyes made a slow sweep upwards from her bare feet, and the pink-painted toenails—presumably the sandals dangling from her fingers belonged there.

Though it looked as if she could not have made less effort, you had to feel sorry for the women who had spent hours getting ready. Angel had stopped short of appearing in her shorts or arriving with a group of salivating half-dressed holidaymakers in tow, but her outfit was more beach than drinks party. Had she deliberately underdressed in order to stand out from the crowd? he speculated. If so, the effort was unnecessary. As the man had said, she would have stood out in every crowd and he doubted any man in the room could find fault with her choice of outfit.

She brought irresistibly to mind the archetypal image of a Greek goddess in the semisheer column that revealed every sinuous inch of her long, shapely legs from calf to thigh. Bare shoulders gleamed gold above the draped fabric that followed the lines of her full, high breasts and was cinched in beneath by a tie before flowing out in long, soft folds.

The fabric shimmered, Angel shimmered.

As far as he could tell she was wasn't wearing a scrap of make-up. Her face, with the full sexy mouth, cute nose and spectacular dark-lashed eyes, was beautiful, framed against a silken fall of river-straight hair that dropped to her waist.

Luckily, Angel thought, when reliving the moment later that night, she'd had a drink already thrust into her hand when the billionaire who had granted them exclusive use of his private island to film the series of commercials was pointed out to her.

'Now, that's what I call a face.'

If only she'd had some warning, some inkling. But then that was, she supposed, the definition of shock, and it hit Angel like a sudden immersion into icy water. Initially her mind went utterly blank, rejecting what she was seeing. Then the breath froze in her lungs; there was a solid block of ice in her chest. Was this a panic attack? she wondered, feeling like a drowning man going down for the final time as she struggled to mask her feelings, willed her face to stay blank.

She looked away and waited for the pounding throb of her heart to slow. Her first instinct had been to run, but that was not an option given her limbs were not acting as though they belonged to her, except for her hand, the one with the glass in it, which managed to find her mouth.

She swallowed the contents in one gulp, her eyes darting from side to side like a trapped animal. There was no place to hide and he was coming her way. Without looking, she could sense his approach.

How was she acting so normally?

She even managed to say something to Sandy, the pretty make-up artist who had initially pointed Alex out to her. What it was Angel had no idea, but she must have been funny because the other girl laughed. *That's me, funny Angel, smart Angel, lucky Angel... Scared witless Angel!*

'Are you cold? You're shivering.' The other girl sounded worried.

Angel swallowed and made herself respond to Sandy's concerned question, forcing the words past the constriction in her throat.

'No, I'm not cold.' And she wasn't. The warm glow in her stomach, the combination of champagne and brandy in the cocktail, had begun to seep into her bloodstream. 'That's Alex Arlov?'

Her voice sounded as though it were coming from a long way off. Her head was still spinning as she struggled to take on board the identity of her one-night stand, the father of her child.

Sandy misinterpreted the cause of Angel's stunned expression. 'I know, he looks even better in the flesh, doesn't he? You could cut yourself on those cheekbones.'

The other woman seemed to take it for granted that Angel recognised the billionaire by sight. And Angel did know the name, of course—who didn't? She could even have recited a potted bio of the man, not because she found money sexy or shared the popular fascination with people who had amassed a great deal of it, but because, and here the irony was so black a short, hard cough of laughter escaped her clenched teeth, her brother had tried in his oh-so-not-subtle way to set her up with the man!

The two men had met while both were driving ridiculously fast cars around a racing circuit for fun. Her brother's excuse was it had once been his day job; the other guy, as far as she had been able to tell at the time, had been there because he enjoyed pushing the limits and he could afford the sort of toys that only very rich men could.

The two men appeared to have bonded over a mutual love of speed and obviously wives had not come into the conversation or Cesare would not have tried to set her up with the man. Her brother had been oblivious, of course, to the fact they were discussing the father of her child, and the man her overprotective sibling had, on more than one occasion, expressed a desire to dismember slowly. Angel's response had been firm but dismissive. For Cesare, the habit of watching out for his little sister was deeply engrained.

'I'm not interested in dating a Russian oligarch, even one who drives well in wet conditions,' she'd said.

Her brother had grinned at the retort but protested. 'Not dating—I was simply suggesting we invite him up for the weekend some time. I think you two would get on. He'd get your sense of humour and, let's face it, that puts him in the minority. And he's only half Russian; his father died before he was born and his mother fell out with his family and moved back home. There was a grandfather in Russia, hence the Russian oil, but as his mother was half Greek he was brought up by that side of his family, and actually he's taken British citizenship.'

'Fine, invite him, whatever you like,' Angel had responded, making a mental note to be away any weekend her brother tried to play matchmaker. 'But I think one adrenaline junkie is enough in any family.'

And it had been left at that.

It was her own adrenaline levels that presented the most immediate problem now. Light-headed to the point where she saw black dots dancing, and with her heart thudding like a metronome-driven sledgehammer against her ribs, it was taking a conscious effort to act with anything approaching normality. The muscles in her cheeks burned with the effort of keeping her smile pasted on as she absently licked the crystals of sugar deposited on her lips by the decorated rim of her now-empty glass. She watched him approach... nearer and nearer...

Her galloping paranoia saw something predatory about his long-legged, straight-backed stride. When he got within a few feet of them her stomach went into a steep dive. In other circumstances she would have been riveted, not by fear, but by admiration. Alex Arlov carried himself like a natural athlete, every action screaming fluidity and grace, but also the arrogance that came when someone knew they were at the top of the food chain. Oh, and he could throw a decent pass too; she knew now he had to have been the man she had seen at the beach.

Angel was seized by an irrational certainty that if she took her eyes off him for even a second she would lose her nerve and just bolt...or faint, which would be a first. There had been a close call in the early months of her pregnancy when she hadn't yet realised why she couldn't stand the smell of coffee. She inhaled and closed the door on those thoughts.

By the time Alex had reached them—seconds? Who knew? It was all a blur—Angel had lost the rictus grin of fear and had her face composed into a mask of polite indifference. Bone-deep indifference, though her grip on her composure was not even a cell deep. But who cared as long as she didn't make a fool of herself by giving in to the need to tell him exactly what she thought of him?

The indulgence of venting her real feelings, though tempting, would not exactly improve the situation. Angel knew exactly what she would say. She'd had nearly six years to figure it out, which didn't make her some pathetic creature who'd been unable to move on, or someone who had spent the past six years thinking about him.

She had a life that she loved and he had no place in it. At least that was the way it had worked this morning.... Now he wasn't an unidentifiable figure; he was here and real and present. She had always dreaded the future conversation with Jasmine that began with, 'Sorry, I don't know who your dad is,' but when she thought of naming Alex Arlov as the man in question it suddenly became not such a terrible prospect.

He might not even recognise her...? No such luck, not the way this day was going, she thought, swallowing the bubble of hysterical laughter as she grabbed another drink.

But if he didn't, if he had forgotten she existed the moment he had left the room, would it be so bad to keep him in ignorance? Well, yes, it would be, Angel thought to herself. You could stretch moral ambiguity just so far but it would make life a lot simpler.... She shook her head, unable to deal with the fallout, the deeper implications now. Not falling down was tough enough, she thought, struggling to focus on her contempt and not her near nervous collapse.

Maybe she focused too hard because as his eyes brushed her face for a split second she thought she saw a flicker of shock in those ice-blue depths, but then it was gone and so was his attention.

Angel experienced a weird sense of anticlimax and thought, *Was that it?* Sandy, the recipient of a smile of practised charm, lit up when he spoke to her in the deep gravelly drawl Angel recalled so well. She winced to hear the make-up artist respond with a high girlish giggle, but she couldn't judge. Especially as someone who had gasped *wow* the first time she had seen him was in no position to judge anyone.

The memory made her cringe. Easy hardly covered how very eager she had been to be seduced. She'd been so convinced that she was feeling some deep spiritual connection that he hadn't had to lift a finger to seduce her.

While Alex's attention was on Sandy and she had pulled back from the brink of total panic,

Angel took the opportunity to study him. She wasn't the only one—most of the women in the room were checking him out.

The interest was no mystery—the aura of masculinity that had taken her breath away that first time was still intact, was presumably an integral part of him. He was the sort of man whose testosterone entered the room ahead of him, and, to Angel's intense fury and eternal shame, even after being a victim of it she was still not immune to its effects.

The difference was she was not about to equate her physical response to his blatant sexuality with anything but hormones. The shameful heat between her thighs had nothing to do with love at first sight. She was almost too embarrassed to acknowledge she had ever been naive enough to believe that such a thing existed.

At almost twenty and just starting her art college course, Angel knew she had acquired a reputation for being sophisticated among her fellow students. She never could work out how or why, but the label had stuck.

'You're so independent,' a homesick friend had

once remarked enviously. 'And you can talk to anyone.'

Well, Angel was certainly independent. Arriving home for the school holidays to find a cheque and a note from her mother to explain that she'd been invited to spend the week at a villa in Switzerland made a person independent. And ten schools in eight years made it essential that she could talk to people, though it had been hard on her grades and near impossible to cultivate long-term friendships.

Given her reputation, it was ironic that, unlike most of her contemporaries, at twenty, Angel's experience of the opposite sex had been limited. Her sexual experience had been pretty much nil. Angel's problem had not been low self-esteem or issues about her body or that she was a prude. No, much worse, Angel had been a closet romantic!

The fact was none of the men she had met up to that point had come close to the idealised lover she had imagined was out there waiting for her. And when she'd met the man who looked and acted like her fantasy lover he had turned out to be a lying, cheating rat!

Even though beside her Sandy was still talking, Alex was now staring at Angel. Presumably he thought that money and power negated the need for common courtesy. He probably— The contemptuous observation was not completed because he had her hand in his.... How had that happened?

Myriad half-formed, disconnected thoughts flitted through her head as she stared at his hand, noting with a tightening in her chest that he still didn't wear a wedding band. His brown hands were strong, the fingers long and tapering. Her weirdly heightened senses could make out the slight calluses on his palms. The more she tried not to think about them gliding over her skin, touching her, the more space the images took up in her head.

She squeezed her eyes closed.

Her loss of control could only have lasted a fraction of a second but it felt like a lot longer. When, a moment later, she was able to meet his eyes, what she saw there answered one question—he remembered.

She didn't fall apart. Instead she manufactured a frown as if she were struggling to place him and then widened her eyes and nodded as though she had retrieved the memory she was searching for.

She rewarded herself with the faintest of smiles.

'Alex Arlov.' He tipped his sleek head and to her intense relief released her hand. *How could I ever not have seen how arrogant he is?* She grabbed a napkin from a passing tray and wiped it against the heel of her hand.

'The name seems familiar...' She gnawed lightly on her full lower lip, pretending to search her memory before producing a bright smile and pausing to stretch the moment, hoping like hell he was worrying she was going to out him. If it weren't for Jas she would, and to hell with people knowing what a total fool she was.

But he didn't look concerned, just vaguely amused, as he elevated one dark brow. 'That happens to me all the time—an instantly forgettable face.'

*And so full of yourself,* she wanted to scream as she smiled back, unable to repress a shudder as she looked directly into his ice-blue dark-framed eyes.

She willed herself to relax. Let it go, she told

herself, life moves on. He's just a landmark moment, not a threat.

Her life had moved on, and, if time hadn't completely healed the wounds, it had allowed her to see things from a different perspective. She had made a mistake, but that mistake had given her Jasmine; this man had given her a gift and he didn't know. Jas didn't know either, didn't know who her father was and one day… Did she have to tell him?

'Are you enjoying island life, Miss…?' He arched a brow and studied her. Her features had lost some of their youthful softness, revealing the truly lovely bone structure of her face. She was, he recognised, one of those women who would only improve with age, perfect bone structure compensating for the slight blurring of features as the years passed.

Angel could see his mouth moving, a mouth that was a miracle of stern sensuality, a mouth she had dreamed of. But all she could hear was, *You're married.* Pride had been the only thing that day that had prevented her from crumbling when she had heard him speak the words that had crushed her, words that had turned what she had thought was beautiful into something nasty and sordid.

She blinked and struggled to focus as he repeated himself. Paul, the advertising executive who had followed Alex across the room, caught the question and said, 'We're all on first-name terms here—aren't we, Angel?'

Reminded of a puppy dog eager to please, she flicked a glance his way. She felt sorry for the man, but not as sorry as she felt for herself.... This was a nightmare.

*Breathe,* she told herself. *You've coped with worse.*

Such as once she had got back to her room in the university residence, when she had locked the door and stood under a shower for forty minutes but still hadn't been able to wash off that feeling of self-disgust, shame and the bitterness of disillusion.

Finally she had stopped indulging in the orgy of misery and given herself a stern talking-to.

'What are you going to do, Angel? Stay in here for ever?' Wiping the steam off the mirror, she had glared at her tear-stained face. 'Your problem is you're a dreamer, a stupid dreamer. You wanted deep and meaningful, you wanted to wait, you wanted the first time to be with someone who made you feel special. Well, you didn't get the prince—you didn't even get the frog!' She quite liked frogs. 'So what? Big deal, just suck it up, Urquart.'

It had been good advice then and it still was.

Her chin lifted. 'Angel Urquart, and I'm not actually here to enjoy myself, just to work.' She failed to inject any warmth or animation into her voice, but she managed to deliver the comment with composure. *You're doing well, Angel,* she told herself as she clenched her fingers tight, driving her nails into the softness of her palms.

Now he wasn't touching her she was able to channel some cool of her own. The cool only went skin deep but that didn't matter. What mattered was showing the cheating, lying bastard that there was nothing he could do to hurt her; she had suffered the infection and built up a natural immunity.

'I hope you'll find a little time in your schedule to enjoy what we have to offer, Angelina.'

The predatory gleam in his heavy-lidded eyes shouldn't have shocked her and definitely shouldn't have produced a hot ache at the juncture of her thighs but it did both.

Why surprise? she asked herself. *You jumped into bed with him after five seconds six years ago. Why wouldn't he file you under the heading marked convenient, easy, or most likely both, since you've clearly fulfilled both from his point of view?*

Pushing away the wave of shame, she embraced the anger coursing through her veins. Smiling, she shook back her dark hair and adopted a dumb expression.

'It's Angel, and I'm not actually big on multitasking.' She was confident she could crush his expectations. She might even enjoy doing so. 'You have a beautiful home.'

A home, a wife and to her knowledge at least one child, her child. But for all she knew there could be more, possibly a dozen children…? Did Jasmine have half-sisters, half-brothers…? Not a possibility Angel had considered before, and not one she wanted to consider now!

'This isn't my home. It's a hotel, Miss Urquart.' He paused, the line between his dark brows deepening as he scanned her face. She had gone pale, her full pink lips were blanched of colour and she looked as though she was about to pass out.

'Are you feeling all right?' She heard him ask with more irritation than concern. The rushing sound in her ears made her think of the ocean, which along with a couple of continents was what she needed to put between this man and her before she felt all right. But failing that… She snatched a glass from the tray of a passing waiter, but didn't hold on to it for long.

'I don't think that's a good idea, do you?'

Her green eyes fluttered wide and she stared with utter astonishment as in a seamless motion he tipped the contents of the untouched glass he had taken from her fingers into a flower arrangement. Her jaw dropped as she felt her temper fizz. This man was totally unbelievable!

'What do you think you're doing?' The words didn't deliver the verbal punch she had intended. Instead her voice had a breathy, vulnerable quality. Teeth clenched, she continued to glare up at him, dabbing her tongue to the beads of sweat that clustered along her upper lip. She rubbed a hand across her forearm and found her skin was moist but cold.

He did not enter the debate but, after subjecting her to a narrow-eyed scrutiny, concluded with an air of resignation, 'You need some fresh air.' When he had contemplated her horizontal, a dead faint and ambulances had not entered the picture. So much for a little light flirtation. Alex preferred the woman in his bed to be sober and fully conscious!

He kept telling her what she needed—that night he had known what she'd needed before she had, and he had given it to her. She stiffened as she felt a hand in the middle of her back.

'What do you think you're doing?'

'You are repeating yourself and, in reply… Excuse me…' The small group parted like the sea in response to his soft-voiced request. 'I am saving you from yourself.'

*You're six years too late for that,* she thought, deciding that struggling to evade him would just draw people's attention. As it was she was conscious in the periphery of her vision of a few curious looks as they moved towards the door.

Outside he spoke to a hovering member of staff and a chair appeared. He pressed her down into it. 'Better?'

She nodded and turned her face to the sea breeze. 'It was a bit warm in there.' Actually it was warmer outside but she no longer felt as if the room were closing in on her. Once her head stopped spinning and the tightness in her chest eased she would be fine. 'Thank you. Don't let me keep you from your guests.'

# CHAPTER THREE

'YOU ARE BEING irritatingly childish.'

This lofty condemnation brought her head up with a jerk...mistake! Angel closed her eyes and waited for the world to stop spinning, opening them a moment later when she found a glass placed at her lips. She responded to the terse instruction to drink; the alternative would have been choking because he did not have what could be termed a gentle bedside manner!

She turned her head away and mumbled, 'Enough.'

'You are welcome.' He watched as she dabbed the back of her hand to the excess moisture on her lips and his focus slipped as the memory surfaced of them softening and parting beneath his. The muscles in his angular jaw tensed and the sinews in his neck stood out as he forcibly ejected the memory, but not before he heard the throaty sound of her plea—*please...!*

That husky plea had been all it had taken to silence the voice in his head, the one that had been telling him he ought not to be doing this.

He had done it and he wanted to, needed to, again. The struggle then like now had been to keep his passion on a leash. Something about this woman seemed to tap directly into his primal instincts.

'What happened in there?'

*My past came back to bite me.* 'Other than you overreacting,' she accused him, not willing to admit how close she had come to passing out in public. 'I've told you it w—'

His cold eyes narrowed with irritation as he cut across her impatiently. 'It wasn't the heat.'

She narrowed her eyes and fixed him with a glare. Anyone with an ounce of sensitivity would have tactfully gone along with the heat excuse and not pried and prodded. 'Do we have to have a post-mortem? I got a bit light-headed. It happens. Now I feel much better. I'll have an early night.'

Perhaps the problem was that she had had too many early nights... The thought did not improve his frame of mind. While he was not looking for a long-running thing—there seemed little point

waiting for boredom to set in, as it always did—
he did like exclusivity.

He was not a possessive man but sharing was
a deal breaker.

'It does not happen for no reason.'

Angel started to feel guilty as he continued to
scrutinise her face as though he would find the
answer there.

'Will you stop looking at me like that?' she
husked. 'You're making me feel like a criminal.
I haven't broken any law.'

'Are you sure?'

'I think I'd have remembered.'

'Have you taken anything?'

Still taking breaths of fresh air to clear the
muzziness in her head, she flashed him a confused look, then, as his meaning suddenly
dawned on her, lost all colour. The heat returned
in a searing wave of outrage until her smooth
cheeks glowed.

And the insults just kept coming!

'You're accusing me of being a...a...a...junkie!'
And then he had the cheek to look astonished
when she got upset. This man really was outra-
geous, she fumed.

He felt relief. Her outrage might be a case of the lady protested too much but his instincts told him otherwise. 'No need to overreact.'

She clenched her teeth. The pat-you-on-the-head, patronising quality of his drawled response made her want to scream.

'I'm simply excluding possibilities before I call a doctor.'

Her eyes widened this time in horror. 'I do not need a doctor and I'm not overreacting. I'm reacting to you insulting me, interrogating me...'

'Insult...?' he drawled, his ebony brows lifting at the suggestion. 'It is not exactly unknown in the world you work in for people to...dabble.'

Her mouth twisted into a scornful smile. 'Now, that's what I admire—a man who isn't afraid to generalise or judge from his secure position of moral superiority.'

Alex blinked. She had claws and a mouth on her, this woman—a million miles from the two-dimensional sexy purring kitten of his memory. A slow, contemplative smile spread across his lean, hard face. These changes didn't make her any less attractive, just more of a challenge.

And he had always liked a challenge, or he

had once. Recently he had gone for the easy option way too often, as it came with the lack of emotional commitment that was essential to him. To commit yourself to someone and risk losing them, risk losing part of yourself… A man who invited such a thing more than once was to his mind insane.

'You are clearly feeling better. Actually I was thinking prescription drugs. They can react badly when combined with alcohol.' He tilted his head in the direction of the room they had just exited. 'And you were knocking it back a bit in there.'

So not only was she some sort of junkie, he was also calling her a lush!

'Thanks for the advice.' Her green eyes glowed with contempt, aimed partly at herself. This hypocritical self-righteous creep was the man she'd waited for? She gave a short bitter laugh. Had she really been that young and stupid?

'For the record, being a model doesn't mean I'm part of some seedy subculture. I'm used to people making assumptions—the odd male who thinks that because I've advertised underwear I have no problem with being looked at as though I'm a piece of meat on a slab…' She left a significant pause and had the pleasure of seeing a muscle in his lean cheek clench. 'Not one of the perks of the job,' she conceded. 'However, you have taken insults to a new low. For the record, if I want advice on the clean life I wouldn't come to you, Mr Arlov. You're a…a… Not a nice man.' *Not nice? You're* so *hard core, Angel.* 'You're a rodent!'

As she finished on a breathless note of quivering contempt a memory surfaced as strong as it was unbidden: the ferociously strong lines of his face relaxed in sleep, the long eyelashes softening the angle of his carved cheekbones. Not vulnerable and not soft but more… She had never been able to put a name to the quivering sensation in the pit of her stomach. No more could she now, though she felt it again.

Alex's nostrils flared as he sucked in an outraged breath. He liked feisty but there were limits. 'And you base this opinion on what?'

'That you're a rodent?' She was already regretting the rather limp animal analogy. If there was an animal she would have likened him to it would have been a wolf, with its piercing eyes, sleek, lean body and dangerous bearing. An illicit little shiver slipped slowly like a cold finger down her spine.

'I've always thought rats got a bad press, but not nice? I'm hurt,' he mocked. Alex could live without being thought nice.

'Rodent works for me, but what would you call a married man who sleeps around? For the record, and to save you the effort, these days it takes more than being told someone *needs* me to get me into bed!'

Even if the person saying the words had a voice that was sin itself.

Six years was a long time and people change but this…! 'Thanks for the heads up,' he murmured, adding without missing a beat, 'What does it take?'

She shook her head, playing dumb because it was on the tip of her tongue to admit not much. It was true, and she was ashamed she had recognised him as her moral Achilles the second he had touched her. It had shocked her so deeply it had triggered the… Whatever it had been, Angel remained reluctant to assign a name to what had happened. She was perfectly willing to accept that panic attacks existed; they simply didn't happen to her.

'What does it take to get you into bed these days?' Whatever it was it would definitely be worth the effort. He had not been this hungry for a woman in a long time—if ever.

'I'm curious—do you work at being offensive or are you naturally gifted that way?'

'You didn't answer my question. On second thought, don't. Let me get there by myself. It will be more satisfying than being fed the answer.'

The colour flew to her face. The effects of his purred remark on other parts of her anatomy were too mortifying to think about. 'You're not getting anywhere with me.'

'Oh, well, you know what they say—it's all about the journey not the destination...' A saying that had always struck Alex as particularly ridiculous, never more so than in this context. He had every intention of reaching, enjoying and extracting every atom of pleasure from his destination. The anticipation of sinking into her warm body and losing himself was strong enough to taste.

She shot him a look of utter disdain. 'Do you ever listen to anything anyone says?'

He elevated a dark brow and gave a slow smile. Without a word he hooked his hand behind her head and dragged her face up to his. The action was deceptive, the kiss druggingly deep, his tongue sliding between her parted lips while his firm mouth fitted perfectly over hers. Angel registered the heat that was everywhere; she heard the almost feral low moan but didn't connect the sound with herself.

When it stopped and she managed to prise her heavy eyelids open she found herself looking up into a pair of blazing cosmic-blue eyes. So dizzy she staggered, she gave a choked gasp of horror and stepped backwards, once, twice and amazingly stayed on her feet.

'The truth?'

As if she were emerging from a nightmare—one she had shamefully fully cooperated with and not struggled to escape—Angel fixed her blazing eyes on his face, swallowed a bolus of acrid self-disgust and wiped her hand across her pumped-up plump lips. Where was her self-respect? Where was her pride? When this man touched her she stopped being… She stopped being herself and became someone that scared her, someone whose actions she couldn't predict.

She took a deep restorative breath; she would not fall apart. Yes, he'd like to… But no way. He was acting as if it was no big deal and so could she. It was just a pity the message of defiance had not reached her trembling limbs or core temperature.

'You,' she contended contemptuously, 'wouldn't know the truth if it bit you!' Rich coming from someone who wasn't telling him he had a daughter, or couldn't admit she wouldn't fight too hard if he decided to kiss her again. She lowered her eyes over the shamed acknowledgment and heard his throaty chuckle.

'The truth is I'm more into body language.' Especially when the body in question was as lush and perfectly formed as hers. 'Words can lie… whereas there are some things that you can't hide….'

Her head came up with a guilty jerk. 'I'm not trying to hide anything.' The moment the words left her lips she knew silence would have been more convincing.

'For instance, your pupils have expanded so

much there is just a thin ring of colour left.' Her eyes were the purest green he had ever seen flecked with tiny pinpoints of swirling gold. 'You really are a very good kisser.'

So long as his observations did not drop below neck level she could deal. 'Kissing is not hard.' It was the knowing when not to that was hard. 'It's a…a…reflex,' she flung back.

His ebony brows lifted. 'I've never heard it called that before.'

Hating the smugness in his voice, she snapped. 'You think you know body language? Well, study this,' she invited, pointing to her own face, pale now and set into a cold mask. 'I was ill in that room because I saw you and was reminded of an episode in my life I'm not too proud of, in fact I'm deeply ashamed of.'

'That's your problem, not mine.' Shame and guilt were not to his mind something to be yelled about. They were things you lived with; they were the price you paid for mistakes.

Angel drew in a deep shuddering breath and revealed the ultimate unforgivable crime that she laid at his door. 'You turned me into the other woman.' Her voice dropped to an emotional whisper as she realised. 'You turned me into the person I never wanted to be—my mother!'

Alex's jaw clenched but his anger almost immediately faded. He was very good at reading body language but it did not require his talent to interpret the expression in her emerald eyes as shock.

So Angel had mother issues? That was not his problem, and he had no interest in helping her work her way through them. He refused to recognise an uncharacteristic urge to draw out more details, an urge that directly contradicted his determined lack of interest.

*Six years, Angel, but you got there in the end.* How could she not have seen it before? *'Madre di Dio!'* she mocked softly, then gave a little laugh.

The throaty exclamation distracted him. 'Italian?'

She blinked as it took her a few moments to return from wherever she had gone. 'Half.' She didn't elaborate. It seemed, Angel thought grimly, that she had done too much show and tell already!

Economy of detail was something Alex appreciated in his lovers, actively encouraged, but even he liked a whole sentence.

Well, at least the Latin connection explained

the golden glowing looks, and possibly the temper too, though if he said so she would probably not waste the opportunity to accuse him of generalising.

'I've heard of people rewriting history but this is the first time I've seen it firsthand. You're acting as though you were some passive victim. The way I recall it you were an equal and active participant, so the outraged-virgin act is a bit over the top.' Although amazingly she retained the ability to blush like one—the colour that washed over her cheeks deepened the pale gold of her skin with a rosy sheen. 'This can't be the first time you've bumped into an old one-night stand?'

Her eyes slid from his as she swallowed the insult, though she doubted he had intended it as such. He wasn't making a moral judgement. That was just who he thought she was. It was easier to let him continue to hold that opinion than tell him the truth.

What would be his reaction, she wondered, if she came out with, 'You're the only man I've ever slept with'? She almost laughed at the image of his imagined incredulity. Or worse, he might ask her the question she'd asked herself a thousand times—why him?

How could she begin to explain to him something she didn't even understand herself?

She made herself look at him and felt her insides shudder as their eyes connected. 'One like you.'

In case he decided to construe her comment as a compliment she added coldly, 'One who made me feel…cheap.' Feeling this was an admission too far, she dodged his gaze and missed the expression that flickered across his lean face. When she raised her eyes his face was stone. 'I may just be a model, which clearly in your eyes makes me a pill-popping bimbo—' she took a deep breath and made a conscious effort to control her indignation '—but I don't sleep with married men!'

Her shrill accusations might not have touched him but this last quiet comment did. 'I'm not married now.'

Was that meant to make her feel better? Or was it a lie to get her into bed? Angel told herself she didn't want to know; all she wanted was to get out of here and away from him.

'Now, why doesn't that surprise me?' she

drawled. 'I really hope she took you for a lot of money…' His bank balance was probably the only vulnerable area he had, she thought bitterly.

'She's dead.'

The blunt pronouncement drew a gasp from Angel, who immediately felt like a total bitch. So this was what it felt like to have the rug pulled out from under your feet.

During the ensuing silence the mortified colour flew to her cheeks and then receded. What was she meant to say that didn't sound trite and insincere?

'Oh!'

Before she had said anything more the uniformed employee who had brought her the chair reappeared, this time carrying a tray with a cafetière and coffee cups, and at a nod from Alex he placed it on the table.

The young man spoke in Greek and Alex Arlov responded in the same language.

Questions flying around in her head, Angel watched as he poured the coffee and pushed one her way without asking. Had he loved his wife?

His expression wasn't giving any clues and in her book a man who loved his wife was not unfaithful. *But that's just me, the idealist,* she thought with a wry grimace.

'Do you want sugar?'

Angel, who hadn't been aware she'd been stirring the coffee, put the spoon down with a clatter in the saucer and shook her head. 'No, I don't take it.'

He had slept around, but she supposed that some men did and some women put up with infidelity or didn't know. It was weird to her— Actually, no, it was utterly abhorrent, but marriage meant different things to different people.

'I'm sorry, I didn't know about your wife or I wouldn't have said…what I did.' Then, aware that her comment might come across as hypocritical, she added, 'Even if it is true.'

Had the poor woman lived her life in ignorant bliss, or turned a blind eye, or had she known and cared and suffered the humiliation…? Angel didn't know which scenario was worse.

She tore her eyes from his handsome patrician profile and thought how hellish it must be to be married to a man that other women lusted after. That was one hell she was never going to know about.

Marriage to any man was not on the cards for her. These days, when it was easy to live together—and even easier to drift apart—it seemed to Angel that desire to raise a family was one of the main reasons that couples made their relationship official.

For her there would be no more children. There had been a time when the knowledge had made her sad…angry…filled with a 'why me?' self-pity, but now she had reached a stage of why not me? She had accepted it, and could not imagine a man or a circumstance that would make her walk down the aisle.

She had not discounted the possibility in the future of a man, someone nice who Jasmine liked, someone who didn't make any demands. She could live without head-banging sex but a hug would be nice, and stability. She could remember craving boring stability when she was a child and envying her friends who had complained about the boredom of the things she had longed for.

The expressions scudding like clouds across her face made him wonder what thoughts were responsible for putting that pensive look in her eyes. Then, catching himself wondering, he experienced a flash of irritation.

It seemed a good moment to remind himself that he wanted to bed her, not know how her mind worked.

'I seem to have put a damper on the conversation.'

Her green eyes lifted from the contemplation of the untouched swirling liquid. 'Sorry if I'm not amusing you.' Presumably, she brooded, he was one of those men who expected women to tie themselves into knots being interesting and amusing. 'And we were not having a conversation.' Her eyes lowered towards her coffee and lifted again suddenly. It was as if her resolve not to show any interest broke at the last moment. 'Was it... Your wife... Did she... Did it happen recently?'

'No, it didn't.'

When he offered no further information Angel took a sip of the coffee and looked at him over the rim of her cup. 'It must be hard bringing up children alone...?' she murmured, trying hard not to look like someone who had a stake in his response.

Was Jasmine an only child or did she have half siblings? The brother or sister that Angel had always felt vaguely guilty for not supplying. Siblings looked out for one another when things got tough. If she vanished… Angel gave herself a sharp internal shake. Nothing was going to happen to her, and if it did she had things organised. But a father had not featured in those arrangements.

Of course, if it turned out he had his own family he might not be interested in pursuing a relationship with Jasmine anyway. His loss, though from a selfish point of view it would make life simpler. She felt a stab of guilt. This wasn't about simple, this was about what was best for Jasmine, and if that involved allowing her father to be part of her life she would move heaven and earth to make it happen. He was right; she was no innocent victim. If she hadn't thrown herself at him the way she had none of this would have happened.

She pressed her fingers to her temples. Her head felt as if it would explode with all the unanswered questions swirling round in it, and there were not going to be any of the answers she wanted until she told him.

'We didn't have any children.'

They had planned to have a family but not immediately. Of course, it had seemed as if they would have all the time in the world, then all too soon they had had none. A blessing, Emma, struggling to come to terms with the rapid progress of her illness, had said, but as her denial had turned to deep depression she had become angry and blamed him for... Well, pretty much everything, until it had reached the point when she had turned her head to the wall when he walked into the room.

The doctors had sympathised and called it transference. His wife, they said, was transferring all the guilt she felt for concealing her illness when they married onto to him, and as they had predicted the phase passed. But to his way of thinking what followed was harder. Emma had been consumed with guilt. The precious time they'd had left together had been dominated by it.

Angel lowered her eyes but not before he glimpsed the moisture lingering there and her expression. He reacted to the sympathy he loathed using a tried-and-tested method to kill off the pity that made his skin crawl.

'Turn down the empathy, Angel. I'm not a candidate for a sympathy shag,' he drawled.

Her appalled eyes flew to his face, suddenly minus their emotional moisture. 'You are a candidate for a kick,' she retorted, adding in a conversational tone, 'You really can be vile.' She was almost immediately hit by a wave of remorse, so added, 'I am genuinely sorry about your wife.'

'But I'm vile—a rodent, yes, I get that.' The tension vanishing from his manner along with her sympathy, he produced a mocking grin. 'I'm enjoying living down to your expectations of me. Relax,' he advised, 'I do not require a shoulder to cry on.' Though a warm breast to lay his head against would not be rejected. The one in question rose and fell revealing a glitter of something shiny in the deep valley.

'I was not about to offer one.' Offering anything to the only man you had ever fantasised about lying naked beneath was something to be actively avoided. She swallowed hard and dropped her gaze, wishing she had not thought about being naked. 'And I have no expectations.'

'But some curiosity.' The speculation was pretty much proved when she couldn't meet his eyes. 'Don't feel bad. Everyone wants to ask. Few do—death is one of those subjects that people tiptoe around. Emma died of MS, an aggressive form she had been ill with for some time.'

Angel could only marvel that he could sound so detached while revealing this tragic sequence of events. For all the emotion he was displaying he could have been recounting the story of a stranger's life.

'It was lucky we had no children.' He sketched a sardonic smile. 'Now your turn...?'

She got that he rejected sympathy—hard not to—but she felt it anyway, a strong surge of empathy that she couldn't repress. She would have felt the same for anyone in his situation; the difference was she hadn't spent the past six years hating anyone. Not to do so, even briefly, felt odd...uncomfortable, and required some major mental readjustment.

'One.' She couldn't pretend that Jasmine didn't exist.

He stiffened. 'In most countries that is all a person can have at one time.' The joke, it seemed, was on him. Why the hell hadn't she just told him she was married up front?

*Why didn't you consider the possibility, Alex?*

Her bewildered-sounding response cut across his inner dialogue. 'One…?'

'You're not wearing a ring,' he clenched out, feeling cheated.

Anchoring her hair against a sudden flurry of wind, she followed the direction of his gaze and drew the hand down to look at it, turning it over as she blew away the errant raven strands that immediately plastered themselves across her face. She was of the school of thought that said less was more when it came to jewellery and she rarely wore rings when working. Her hand went to her neck where she wore her father's signet ring on a chain. Her brother had inherited a Scottish estate complete with castle, and she, being a woman, had got only the ring. She didn't resent it half as much as her brother felt guilty about it.

'Why should I…?' She stopped as the penny dropped. 'God, not a husband! I have a child, a daughter.'

This was only slightly less astonishing to him than her having a husband. His eyes went to the fingers that were rubbing the chain she wore around her neck. Through her fingers he recognised the disc he had initially taken for a pendant nestled between her breasts as a ring.

'You have a baby?' His eyes drifted down her slim body and he felt a kick of lust that made his strong-boned features clench.

Hard not to recognise this as the perfect opportunity to speak. *So why aren't you, Angel?*

*We have a baby.* It didn't matter how hard she tried, Angel couldn't visualise his reaction to this bombshell.

'She's hardly a baby.' Her expression softened. Jasmine had been a lovely baby, though it might have been easier to enjoy her loveliness if she had ever slept. The first eighteen months had passed in a blur of sleep deprivation.

'But she must be young, and you're a single parent…?' Did the ring have some significance? A token from the father?

Angel instantly prickled with antagonism; her chin went up. She was pretty secure when it came to her parenting skills, able to shrug off and smile her way through well-meaning advice, but when the source of the criticism was the absent father of her daughter it turned out she couldn't.

'Yes, I am, and I really don't think my childcare arrangements are your concern,' she tossed back, realising as she spoke that this situation might change very soon. When he knew he might think that he should have a say. The idea appalled her.

Blinking at the level of belligerence in her attitude, he made a pacifying gesture with his hands. Her eyes followed the gesture—he had lovely hands.

'I am hardly an expert on the subject.'

He watched as her hunched shoulders flattened. He could almost feel her willing the tension away. Her tense smile was a clear effort and she avoided his eyes. 'That doesn't stop most people offering advice.'

'Is her father involved?'

Angel couldn't look at him. Lucky thing she was sitting down because her knees were shaking. 'No.'

'I imagine it can't be easy...?'

He imagined right, but Angel would not have it any other way. The sleepless nights were more than compensated for in a million other ways. 'I make it work.'

'I'm sure you do.'

Again, she couldn't take his comment at face value. 'And no, I'm not naive enough to think a single working parent can have it all, but I don't want it all.'

From this defiant statement he read that she wanted it but couldn't have it. The idea that the father was unavailable, most likely married, seemed a real contender. Funny how some women were drawn to unavailable men.... Was she one of them?

'We all want some things more than others.' And at that moment all he wanted, wanted so much he could taste it, was this provoking, dark-haired, green-eyed witch. His innate ability to distance himself from a situation had failed him completely—he wanted her under him, he wanted to be inside her and he knew he wasn't going to have a moment's peace until he had achieved this desire.

The expression in his eyes stopped her asking what it was he wanted more than other things. The expression in his blue eyes was explicit enough to cause a head-on collision between a fist of some unidentifiable emotion and her solar plexus.

She got to her feet. 'Well, thanks for the coffee and the little chat but I'm fine now.'

'I'll walk you back to your bungalow.'

A cold fist of fear tightened in her belly as Angel realised that she wanted to say yes. When she recognised how much she wanted to say yes the fist tightened even more.

She tossed back her hair and made her voice cold. 'That will be quite unnecessary and I'm not going back to my bungalow. I'm going back to the party.' A room full of people no longer seemed a bad thing; she didn't want to be alone with her thoughts.

'If it makes you feel any better, Emma, my wife, died several weeks before we slept together.'

The words stopped her in her tracks. She shook her head. Was she being slow...? 'You expect that to make me feel better?'

He had, but it was fairly obvious he had been wrong. 'I thought you had a right to know.' The comment had not sounded so lame or pompous in his head.

'But not before I spent six years worrying that I'd turned into my mother. Why on earth did you say you were married?'

'I didn't say, you assumed.'

'And you didn't put me right. Why… Oh, you… Oh…' Comprehension flickered into her eyes. 'It was the quickest way to get rid of me…?'

'I have a distaste of scenes.'

She sucked in a deep breath through flared nostrils. Hearing the beat of helicopter blades somewhere in the distance she could only hope that they were here to whisk him away. 'I'm going back into the party—your party, so I can't stop you coming too, but if you pester me so help me I'll report you to the hotel management for harassment and I don't care who it upsets!'

Not him, if his expression was any indicator. 'I can speak for the management when I say that we take all complaints very seriously.'

'We?' She shook her head. 'This hotel is part of the Theakis group.' Her frown deepened as his firm lips twitched. 'What is so funny? Don't you believe I would?'

'Oh, I believe you would follow through with any rash threat you make. But before you do I should explain that my grandfather was Spyros Theakis, Angelina. I *am* the Theakis group and speaking in that role I can assure you we take all such complaints very seriously.'

The realisation hit Angel like a stone. Having deflated her, he strode off in the opposite direction without another word or backwards glance.

# CHAPTER FOUR

ANGEL STAYED AT the party for another hour but by the time she reached her room her headache had become a full-blown migraine. At least it meant she wasn't going to lie awake going over the events of this evening. Instead, she was going to lie awake waiting for the medication, which she always carried with her, to kick in, willing herself not to throw up while she tried to ignore the vice crushing her skull and the metronome inside it.

Wow, it was a win-win situation!

She did throw up. In fact she spent half the night with her head in the toilet. It had been after four when she had finally crawled back to bed and fallen asleep, a fact that resulted in her spending an age in Make-up—or maybe that was normal for film? Angel didn't have a clue and as she stepped out in front of the camera she was very conscious of her inexperience.

She told herself that no one wanted her to fail, but she could imagine a few people might be amused if she did. As it was, she didn't mess up. Apparently the first full morning's filming had gone well, though to Angel the progress had seemed torturously slow.

She said as much to her co-star, if that was the right description of the actor who was to play opposite her in the soap-style series of adverts.

'Take up knitting like me, darling,' he advised.

'How long do you think we have for lunch?'

'In my humble opinion…' he began.

Angel couldn't not smile. In her opinion Clive didn't have a humble bone in his body.

'All right, not so humble.' He might not do humble, but he did have a sense of humour. 'We have finished for the day.'

It turned out he was right.

Angel had already checked it out so she knew that the narrow strait of water that separated the private island from the hotel beach was safe. So when she declined a seat on the boat in favour of swimming the short distance her co-star responded in much the same way he had when he'd found her reading a book.

'For pleasure?'

Angel, who knew he had a post-grad degree, suspected he was never off duty, always playing his part as the pretty-but-dim public school boy that most of his well-paid Hollywood roles had involved him playing.

The deep turquoise water was warm and Angel, who was a strong swimmer, was a couple hundred yards from the beach when she stopped and began to tread water, watching the people on the beach before flipping onto her back to float lazily.

It was the angry metallic buzz sound of the Jet Ski that made her lift her head. If she hadn't she wouldn't have seen the kid who had obviously drifted out farther than he intended on an inflatable toy, and she watched in horror as he fell off into the path of the Jet Ski.

Two things became immediately obvious. One, he couldn't swim very well and two, the driver of the Jet Ski couldn't see him.

Her yelled warning alerted the people on the shore, several of whom entered the water shouting, but the Jet Ski rider remained oblivious and she was a hell of a lot closer than anyone else.

With a pounding front crawl that left her breathless, Angel managed to get to the child and make sure he stayed afloat. But it became harder to stay that way when the boy let go of the inflatable and transferred his hold to her neck, gripping tightly. Pulled under without a chance to fill her lungs, she surfaced a few moments later with the kid latched on like a limpet only to see the Jet Ski heading right for them.

At the last moment she pushed the kid's face into her shoulder and closed her eyes, not perhaps the most practical response, but it worked to the extent that they were still alive when she opened them. Though this was, it turned out, less to do with her closed eyes and more to do with the Jet Ski rider seeing them at the last moment.

He swerved and didn't quite miss them. But her shoulder only took a glancing blow, which she barely noticed, as at this point she was busy struggling to stay afloat. The kid was half strangling her with his grip, and the close encounter with the Jet Ski had seriously freaked him out so he had begun kicking out wildly with his legs.

The relief when a speedboat pulled up alongside and someone hauled him up out of her arms was intense.

'Thank you so much.' Her grateful waterlogged smile faded slightly when she saw the owner of the hand she had grabbed gratefully on to, his face a dark shadow against the sun shining directly into her eyes. But there was no mistaking his identity.

She landed in the boat in a staggeringly inelegant, breathless heap and crawled onto a bench seat.

'You're all right?'

'Fine,' she lied, finding herself nodding meekly in response to his stern, 'Don't move.' As if she could have if she'd wanted to!

Alex didn't trust himself to respond to this patent lie and maintained his silence on the way back to shore, choosing not to compete with the boy, who was now bawling in his ear very loudly.

'I want my mum.'

'She is welcome to you.'

Angel gasped. 'Don't be so mean. Can't you see that the poor thing is upset?'

*He* was upset! Alex was pretty sure that watching her swim directly into the path of that Jet Ski had taken six months off his life. Angel, on the evidence so far, was not destined to make it to thirty!

'I can *hear* that he's upset,' Alex retorted grimly, holding the kid with one hand and steering the boat with the other. He flashed her a look of irritation and snarled, 'Will you sit still? Because if you fall out, so help me I'll let you drown. In all my life I have never witnessed such a reckless, suicidal, stupid action!' he raged. 'Every time I see you, you are trying to kill yourself!'

Before she could defend herself against this unjust attack he cut the engine and the people who had waded out into the shallows were there, arms outstretched, to deliver the boy to his mother.

A young man wearing the logo of the hotel on his polo shirt and a label that identified him as a lifeguard on his cap climbed into the boat and, after speaking to Alex, took the wheel.

Alex himself peeled off his own shirt, dived neatly into the water from the far side of the boat and vanished under it before appearing on the shore side where the water reached his waist.

Hair slicked wetly back, looking like some impossibly perfect front cover of a men's health magazine, he squinted up at Angel, water streaming down his brown face. 'Do you want someone to take you to the marina or...?' He held out a hand.

She treated his offer of assistance from the boat with a look of cold disdain, though as she lowered herself into the water the pain in her shoulder made her wish she had swallowed her pride.

He didn't turn back once to see if she was managing so it became a matter of pride that she stay on her feet even though a delayed reaction to the drama was beginning to set in.

When she reached the shore slightly distant from the group around the child and his family, she watched Alex in action. He took charge, of course he did—it was clearly second nature to him. He was just one of those individuals people naturally turned to in times of crisis and he was good, she had to admit, as she watched him soothe, calm and casually issue instructions.

It was curious that the father of the child who had up until that moment held it together broke down and started weeping, almost as if Alex's competence gave him permission to fall apart.

At that point his wife stopped crying and began berating their son, who had been on the point of enjoying all the attention.

'If it hadn't been for that lady…. She's a hero-ine.'

Someone clapped and someone else picked it up, then with a chain-reaction effect the ripple spread and everyone was clapping.

Angel, whose entire attention had been focused on Alex—she might even have had her mouth open—became belatedly aware of people look-ing in her general direction, and looked around expecting to see the heroine referred to until the penny dropped…. *Oh, God!*

With heaven-sent timing the shaken driver of the Jet Ski chose this moment to wade ashore and, taking advantage of the distraction af-forded by his appearance, Angel headed for the rocky area that shielded the main beach from the smaller, quieter cove at the far end. She gave a quick furtive look over her shoulder before she waded through the water and then down onto the beach the other side of the rocky outcrop.

The small cove was empty, and with a sigh of relief Angel flopped down onto the sand, her closed eyelids filtering out some of the brutal midday sun. It wasn't until she stretched out that she realised she wasn't only shaking on the inside but on the outside too, fine tremors that shook her entire body.

She lay still and waited for it to pass, nursing her head, which, still tender from the previous night, had begun to throb gently. Great, she needed that like a… Actually a hole in the head might relieve the pressure she could feel building.

Alex was probably the only one who had seen her slip away. He was definitely the only one to follow her. The idea of her acting like some sort of injured animal, crawling away to lick its wounds, made him furious. The woman had the self-preservation instincts of a lemming.

He clambered over the rocks, not around them, to reach the empty cove. There was a very good reason it was empty at this time of day. The water Angel had waded through was already waist deep and in another ten minutes it would be cut off from the bigger beach. Swimming around or a trek through the pine-forested strip that edged the sand were the only ways back to the hotel, a fact that was written in red letters a mile high on signs along the beach.

When he spotted her stretched out on the sand he hit the ground running, then stopped as he saw her chest lift, her breasts pushing against the black fabric of her bikini top.

At the best of times—which this was not—Alex was not well schooled in compassionate concern; he lacked the finesse and the patience. Yet as he reached the spot where she lay and looked down at her he felt his anger slip away. In his head he saw her face when she had realised the applause was for her. Many people dreamed of earning such plaudits, of being hailed a hero, but she had looked…stunned, horrified. It would have been the prefect punishment to have drawn her in to take a curtain bow, but the hunted expression on her face as she had slipped away had made him repress the malicious impulse.

Lying there, she managed to simultaneously look as sexy as hell and damned, throat-achingly vulnerable.

'Are you all right?' Concern added a layer of gravel to his deep voice.

She didn't leap out of her skin, but only because

she had felt his shadow blocking the sun a fraction of a second before he spoke. Still stinging from his unfair comments in the boat, she imagined the expression of impatience on his lean face. In her head she could see him glancing at his watch, thinking, *That bloody woman again!*

She raised herself onto her elbows but didn't lift her gaze. 'I'm fine,' she said, arching her foot to rub the sand off one foot with the red-painted toes of the other.

His eyes on the top of her dark head, he wondered how she managed to make the assurance sound much the same as *go away*—it was a talent. He was sorely tempted to do just that. If she was so determined to put herself in a hospital, who was he to stop her?

Unaware that he had chosen that moment to drop gracefully into a squatting position beside her, Angel started to sit upright. The near collision of their heads drew a tiny gasp of alarm from her throat. Rocking back on his heels, he remained, from Angel's point of view, far too close!

He still didn't have his shirt on, and he made her think of a particularly sexy pirate. How embarrassing that she couldn't stop staring at his chest; her eyes were welded there.

'I'm fine,' she croaked, thinking this comment had rarely in her life been less true.

'You're working on the theory that if you say it more than once it makes it so.' He didn't sound amused; he sounded exasperated.

'It *is* so.' Teeth pressing into the pink softness of her full lower lip, she finally managed to drag her eyes upwards and discovered that he wasn't looking impatient or even angry. He was looking worried and concerned, and instead of being mollified by the discovery she was thrown into an instant state of heart-pounding confusion. With Alex it seemed a condition she spent about ninety per cent of her time in.

From the tangled muddle of emotions lodged like a heavy stone in her chest, anger and resentment dissolved. Without them she felt oddly defenceless; she didn't know how to deal with his concern. *Who are you kidding, Angel? You don't know how to deal with him full stop!* The man was the father of her child and he was a total stranger—a pulse-racingly disturbing total stranger.

Well, one solution would be to get to know him, she thought. He's right here. Stop snarling and start talking. Was picking fights with him a way that she had subconsciously adopted to delay the moment she told him about Jasmine? She tried to push the idea away but it lingered…as did the scent of his soap in her nostrils.

'I really am all right. I was just escaping the fuss.… How about the boy?'

'He doesn't seem any the worse for the experience,' Alex commented drily. 'He was posing for photos when I left.… What's wrong?'

'Nothing.'

'You winced.'

She expelled an exasperated sigh of surrender and snapped. 'My head hurts. It's nothing.' Compared to last night it was true. She turned her head, giving a little grunt of relief when she saw that the skin on her shoulder was not broken. It was sore, though.

Growing irritation made his jaw clench again. She had managed to make it sound as if it were his fault.

'Let me see.'

She turned her head away. 'No, I didn't hit it. I just have a headache.'

'Headaches don't leave bruises.' His long brown fingers, their touch delicate but firm, pushed aside the saturated strands of hair from her forehead, causing her eyes to fly wide and green to his face, the frantic fluttering sensation that began in the pit of her stomach and spread hot and dangerously fast making her pull away while she could.

The subsequent jolt caused her bruised shoulder to ache.

'Leave me alone.'

The words mocked Alex even as her belligerent emerald eyes taunted him.

Leave her alone!

*That's your problem,* Alex thought grimly. *You can't.*

Six years ago he hadn't been able to and he still couldn't. From the moment he had seen her he had wanted her and that hunger had not decreased. If anything it had grown and it didn't matter how aggravating, how sheer bloody minded she was, no negative was negative enough to make him any less hot for her.

Around this woman his self-control was zero. Even the fact she had just been involved in an accident didn't save her from his lust. No, lust he could cope with, but this ability she had to draw emotional responses from him was something he was not willing to recognise, let alone deal with.

'You're bloody lucky all you have is a headache!'

The fresh blast of disapproval hurt but at least it enabled her to throw off the weird feeling of vulnerability.

'Do you have to yell?' She framed a pained furrow between her darkly defined brows. 'I'm not deaf.' Or needy, she reminded herself.

His jaw tightened and the memory of her putting herself between the blades of the Jet Ski and the child resurfaced to increase his rage. 'Do you ever think about the consequences of your actions?'

It was the consequences of both their actions that she had been living with for six years. 'I accept them,' she told him quietly. 'How about you?' Well, she was going to find out the answer to that one very soon.

He ignored the wry interjection and barely registered her sudden look of panic. 'We are not talking about me. I'm talking about your publicity-seeking stunt.'

Her temper fizzed. 'A stunt! You think I arranged that?'

Alex didn't, but the thought had flashed through his mind. 'No, I don't think you've got the brains....' he admitted, an edge of weariness entering his voice as he added, 'Do you ever think before you leap or jump?'

She fixed him with an evil-eyed stare. 'You're right, I didn't think. Story of my life!' She sniffed. 'If I had thought, do you think I'd have wasted my virginity on a selfish, lying bastard who let me think he was married just to get out the door?'

She closed her eyes to blot out the expression stamped on his face. The man didn't just look shocked, he looked as though someone had aimed a loaded revolver at him and pulled the trigger.

The words didn't just hang in the air, they vibrated, the volume growing with each beat of her heart. Unfortunately, there was no way she could retrieve them because, true to form, she'd done it again. She'd blurted out the truth at the worst moment imaginable. *Way to go, Angel, out to personally disprove the old adage that wisdom came with age.*

# CHAPTER FIVE

'YOU'RE TRYING TO tell me… No… No, you were not a virgin!' Even as Alex voiced the denial his brain was making connections that he couldn't believe he hadn't seen before.

''Course not. What can I say? I have a sick sense of humour.'

Angel's eyes were closed, squeezed tight like a little kid who thought the action made her invisible.

'You were.' He dragged a hand through his hair and got to his feet, walking several steps away before stalking back to stand over her. 'You were a virgin, and you acted like a damned…'

'Damned what?' she challenged, getting to her feet.

He just looked at her and shook his head, groaning. *'Theos!'*

She shrugged, wrapping her arms around herself, cold despite the afternoon heat. Shock, she speculated, viewing the tremors that were shaking her body with a weird objectivity. The genie was out of the bottle, the truth was out there and she couldn't get it back, so she did the only thing possible—she downplayed it like mad!

'Let's not make a big deal of it. A girl's got to lose it some time.'

'You think this is a subject for cheap jokes? It *was* a big deal. It *is* a big deal—to me and it should be to you.' He hadn't even been Emma's first lover, and it had not been important to him. For some men perhaps there was an appeal in teaching a novice the ropes, but it was a responsibility that he would have actively avoided had the opportunity ever arisen. It hadn't—or so he had thought.

'I'm sorry if my ability to laugh at ancient history offends you, but it was a long time ago and life moves on.' And it also occasionally threw some surprises, and the surprise today was the strength of Alex's reaction to the news. He was still pale beneath his tan. 'There has to be a first time for everyone—it's the second time that can be more problematic.' She cleared her throat and, regretting the reference to her nonexistent sex life, hurriedly tacked on a laughing, 'Even you.'

She lifted her eyes to his face and her smile faded. It was impossible to imagine Alex being young and inexperienced, his face smooth, his eyes without cynicism.

'Why the hell didn't you tell me?' he blasted.

His indignation continued to strike her as pretty perverse. 'I don't recall conversation being very high on the agenda.' She forced the words past the tight constriction in her throat. 'Would it have made any difference if I'd told you?'

Alex opened his mouth and closed it again. It was a good question and he'd have liked to think it would, but on that day he had not been thinking with his brain.

'I resent being made to feel like some sort of bloody predator.'

*He* resented! 'Well, I'm *so* sorry I've made you feel a victim, but I guess it's a responsibility I'll have to live with.'

The saccharine insincerity dripping from her sarcastic retort brought a defining flash of colour to the knife-edged contours of his carved cheekbones.

'Did you set out that day with the intention of—?' He bit down on the question, but not soon enough to stop Angel's eyes sparking afresh with anger.

'Sure,' she drawled, disguising her hurt with a sarcastic tone. 'I engineered the whole thing.'

A muscle alongside his mouth clenched as their eyes connected, sizzling blue on flashing green. 'You can't leave anything, can you?' he charged. *Like the fact you acted like a total irresponsible bastard, Alex?* 'I know it wasn't your fault,' he gritted through clenched teeth. 'It was my bloody...' He stopped abruptly. 'You said the *second* time was the problem.' He shook his head, not following the crazy idea to its equally crazy conclusion.

'Did I?' she said, thinking did this man miss nothing? She adopted a sweetly insincere smile and hid behind the truth. 'Oh, yes, you've guessed it. You spoiled me for any other man, Alex.'

Responding to her mockery with a curt, unsmiling, 'Except for the father of your child,' he extended a hand to her.

Staring at the hand, not the man she nodded. 'Oh, yes, there is him.' And there was Jasmine.

And Jasmine's father.

Oh, God! She knew the delay with coming clean was not making things better, quite the opposite, in fact. With a sigh she dropped her head into her hands and began to scrub her eyes with the heels of her palms. She felt a surge of despairing disgust as she asked herself where was the woman who never avoided an awkward issue but met it head on?

As she tilted her head to look at him her hair fell back, revealing the beginning of a bruise on her temple. Staring at the discoloration, Alex felt his stomach muscles lurch and tighten with an emotion as strong as his previous anger and totally inexplicable.... Only a madman would feel protective towards this provocative witch with her smart mouth and her combative attitude.

He was not a madman. It was *her* sanity that was the issue here; *her* insane behaviour was what he was here to challenge, although the conversation had drifted somewhat. *Time to refocus, Alex,* he thought.

'That was a crazy thing you did.' Also brave; the private concession was made reluctantly. It was hard not to admire this woman's fearlessness—at least from a distance. For those close to her it must make life hell, he thought grimly. 'You could have killed yourself....'

He closed his eyes, seeing the scene again and experiencing the same awful sense of helplessness. The memory remained like an icy fist in his chest as he glared at her and spelt out the fact she seemed incapable of grasping. 'You could be dead.'

'I can't die. I have Jasmine,' she asserted confidently. It was a simple fact. Jasmine would have been without a mother and that couldn't happen.... It nearly had!

Like a tower of cards her confidence slipped away. Oh, God, he was right. She was a mother—she couldn't go around leaping in without thinking.

'I'm a terrible mother!'

Hearing the anguished wail and seeing the tears rolling silently down her cheeks cut through the righteous anger that gripped him like a hot blade through butter. He was unable and unwilling to identify the emotion that tightened in his chest as tenderness, but he dropped back down beside her. His time when he touched her she did not pull away as though he were poison. Instead she leaned into him, melted into him softly, shaking her head on his chest.

One moment he was fighting the urge to throttle her, the next he was fighting an equally primal desire to comfort her. His emotions did one of those three-hundred-and-sixty-degree shifts that seemed to happen around her.

'What if—?'

'You have lived to tell the tale. There is no point in what ifs. So how old is she, your daughter... Jasmine?' He spoke not out of genuine interest but a need to distract her. At the same time he ran a soothing hand over her wet hair, lifting it off her neck; the texture of her warm, damp skin beneath fascinated him.

'She's started school. Well, she had.'

*'Had?'*

'She was off a term as she wasn't well, but she's having some home tutoring and she'll soon catch up. She's smart.'

The audible pride in her muffled response caused his hand to still, though the dark strands of her wet hair remained coiled around his fingers. It was difficult for him to see her as a mother but, he thought to himself, *You don't have the exclusive on family feeling, Alex.*

'She's better now?' he asked, giving her time to regain control.

Angel nodded into his chest. 'I took some time off but this opportunity was too good—' He felt her stiffen before she pulled away from him. Tucking her hair behind her ears, she regarded him with a defiance that was echoed in her addition. 'I suppose you don't think mothers should work?'

She clearly expected his judgement. *And why not, Alex? You've done little else but judge so far.*

*Quick to judge and slow to forgive.* The words of his mother, a sad observation that he had lived to understand the meaning of but that had meant little to him when she'd spoken them soon after his half-sister had appeared like a disruptive whirlwind in their lives.

'I know nothing of the pressures of being a mother...or a parent.' His brow creased as he admitted, 'I still struggle to think of you as one.'

'A mother or an actual person, not a body that looks good in a bikini?' Before he could respond to the bitter accusation she added wearily, 'Being a mother is one job where experience is not a prerequisite.'

'There's nothing on your website that mentioned you have a daughter. Is that a professional thing?'

'You're not the only one who likes their privacy.' She blinked her sooty lashes over wide emerald eyes as her voice dropped an astonished husky octave. 'You looked me up?'

'I was curious.'

So was she, and maybe it was the hint of evasiveness in his manner but she suddenly heard herself asking the question that she'd heard many people voice, but that as yet had no satisfactory answer. Everyone had theories but nobody could really understand why they were being allowed access to the private island.

'Why *are* you giving us access to Saronia?' The moment the words left her lips she regretted them, but it was too late to back off. 'They say you've refused royal requests.' Why would a man who'd refused honeymooning royals open his doors—or at least a restricted area of his shoreline—to them?

'Do they?'

She narrowed her eyes. 'You know they do.'

'So what is your theory?'

She lifted a hand to shade her eyes. It was a bit late in the day to make out that she hadn't thought about it, but she tried anyway. 'I don't have one, but if I had to guess I'd go with those who think it's a bored, rich man's whim, unless you really are thinking of expanding into cosmetics?' Apparently the rumour had gone viral.

'Are you asking for insider information?'

'Hardly. The rumour has already sent the firm's shares through the ceiling. Even we mere models have been known to read the financial pages,' she observed, quite pleased to have surprised him. Her smug grin vanished as he hitched a brow and, holding her eyes with his, touched the sole of her foot with his finger. The light, barely there contact made her stomach dissolve and her toes curl of their own volition.

'Has no one suggested that it is because I wanted to have you at my mercy?'

She fought against the seductive quality of his deep voice, hating that he was mocking her. 'Now, that really would make me feel special.'

He shrugged and grinned. 'No mystery. My nephew asked me to further his career.'

'And you're a very nice uncle who does favours for your nephew?'

'It has been known, but I am an *adequate* uncle. It isn't hard—Nico is a nice kid, and it pays to keep on the right side of my sister, Adriana.'

'Do you have much family?' she asked, thinking to herself, *You have one more than you think.*

'My parents died some time ago in a car accident. I have two sisters.... There is Adriana—she's ten years older than me.' His mobile lips twisted into a half smile as he surprised her by confiding, 'I was an afterthought.'

'This is Nico's mother?'

He tipped his head in acknowledgment. 'Her husband, Gus, was an international lawyer based in Geneva, but now he runs the Greek operation. They have just the one son.'

'You said you had *two* sisters?'

There was a long pause.

'Lizzie is your age.'

*Lizzie* did not strike Angel as a very Greek or Russian name. 'I thought you said you were the youngest?'

'Lizzie is my half-sister, the result of an affair—actually a one-night stand.' The small shocked sound that escaped her throat awoke him to the fact that he had just revealed more private details in the past thirty seconds than he had in the past... Actually ever. 'The details are not important.' Just the sort of thing that blew a family apart. 'As I said, she is my half-sister, the baby of the family.'

'And you resent her existence?'

The speculation drew a heavy frown and a flash of anger. 'Nobody in the world could resent Lizzie.' Except his mother, who could have but had not.

The softening in his expression when he spoke of his half-sister could not have been feigned. It could be envied, though she was dismayed to discover she did not envy this girl who brought the warmth to his eyes. One thing Angel did not want to be was his sister!

'So your parents' marriage broke down.' Angel, who knew how that felt, was sympathetic.

Being taken away from the only home she had ever known and the father she had adored at age eight had been a trauma that had stayed with

Angel. In her youthful eyes it had seemed as if she was being punished. What other explanation could there be? Her feelings had alternated between guilt for some unknown sin she must have committed and anger at her father for sending her away.

She had been acting up during one of their short visits to their father when her big brother had sat her down and spelled a few facts out.

'You can act like a spoilt brat and ruin our time here or you can enjoy it. This isn't Dad's fault or mine or yours.'

'But Mum doesn't want us!'

'Sure.' Her brother had held the fists that were punching him in sheer frustration and explained quietly, 'But she doesn't want Dad to have us more than she doesn't want us. Do you get it, kiddo?'

Angel had, sort of, in her childish way. 'I think I hate her, Cesare.' She had whispered the confession because she knew this was a bad thing.

Cesare hadn't said she was bad; he had simply shrugged and retorted, 'Why bother? She's not worth it. Just remember when we're old enough she can't keep us and then we can live where we like.'

'Here at the castle with Dad?'

'Sure,' her brother had agreed, handing her a tissue and advising her to wash her face and brush her hair because she looked like a banshee.

'My father betrayed my mother, she forgave him, there was no divorce.' Angel sighed a sad smile, curving her lips as she dragged her thoughts back to the present. They had gone back to the Scottish castle of their childhoods but there had been no Dad. He had died and Cesare had inherited the ailing highland estate along with responsibility for its debts.

'You were lucky.'

His astonished stare fastened on her face as he sneered, 'How do you figure that one?'

'Divorce is not a good thing and a mother who forgives is…' Head tilted a little to one side, she studied his face. 'But you didn't, did you?'

'What?'

'Forgive him.' He was quick to hide it but Angel saw the shock move at the back of his eyes, followed by a cold, closed look.

'It was not my place to forgive.' And now it

was too late to tell the father he had idolised that he understood the weakness… How could he not when he was staring at his own in the face? 'Though, yes, with the arrogance of youth I did judge. Having indulged in a one-night stand, I am in the classic glass-house-stone-throwing position.'

There was a delicious dark irony that he had blamed his father for not taking responsibility for the consequences of his actions…. Unprotected sex—how stupid is that? He heard the scornful words of his younger self and they still had the power to make him flinch.

The only reason he had not found himself in a similar situation was not down to higher moral standards or even basic common sense, but pure luck!

'So it isn't normal— You…you don't—' She broke off, flushing.

'Sleep with women I have just met? Actually no. Though I can understand why you made that assumption given how we met. That makes you unique on two levels—my only virgin and my only one-night stand,' he remarked bleakly. 'How about you?'

'I thought you'd already decided that a model is an easy lay.'

He winced and frowned at the crudity while uneasily accepting its factual accuracy. 'I was not enquiring about your sexual history.'

'Oh, I see, you just want to know the *real* me?' She widened her eyes. 'Where do I begin? My political views or my favourite author? Let's see, I'm a Pisces, I drink too much coffee and my favourite colour is green....'

'Do you always make a joke when things get too personal?'

Shocked that he had recognised the self-defence mechanism so easily, she shook her head in an angry negative motion, but before she could follow up with a firm denial he asked a question that, even though she knew was inspired by idle curiosity not suspicion, almost tipped her over into outright panic.

'Where is she, your daughter, now?'

Not here, thank goodness.... Angel shuddered to imagine how she would have reacted if fate had thrown this man in her path when Jas had been with her.

'At home, in Scotland, with Ce...' She stopped,

remembering that he knew Cesare and not wanting him to make the link between her and her brother until she was ready. 'I always know she's safe with him.'

The mention of the other man and the perceptible loosening of the tension in her body language when she mentioned him caused muscles along Alex's taut jaw to clench.

He rarely found himself taken by surprise but he was. Having established that the father was not involved in the upbringing of the child, it had not occurred to him to question whether another man was. And considering he was a man who was justifiably famed for factoring in all possibilities when he approached a project, in retrospect it seemed astonishing that he had not foreseen any other outcome, when engineering a situation where their paths would cross, other than them falling into bed together. He had not been willing to contemplate failure.

It had genuinely not once crossed his mind that Angel might be with someone. He struggled to readjust to these facts.

While he recognised it was totally irrational, he could not shake the feeling of being cheated.

*So what did you expect, Alex—that she'd spent the past six years waiting for you to reappear?* The glaring immaturity of his reaction annoyed him, and, continuing in the immature mindset, he found himself blaming her for the situation.

His slightly narrowed eyes went to her left hand, but the long tapering fingers were bare of everything but sand. To leave a child with some-one implied a great deal of trust but there was no ring. He half closed his eyes but he could still see her fingers on his skin. He inhaled and fought his way through a rush of hot lust…*a virgin*!

He still could not get his head round the fact that the best sex in his life had been with a vir-gin! Everything was successfully conspiring to up his guilt levels: the wife he had watched suf-fer barely in the ground and he had jumped into bed with a green-eyed witch…then that tempt-ress had turned out not to be a siren but a vir-gin! Effectively making him feel like some sort of predatory sleaze. What was it they said—ig-norance was no excuse in the eyes of the law?

It was certainly no excuse in his eyes.

He had been staring so long at her hands that Angel had to fight an impulse to hide them. In-

stead she dug them into the sand before rubbing them against her thighs and dragging them
through her wet hair.

'You're with someone?'

This was good, he told himself. It was always
good to focus on a known quantity. A partner
meant there was no chance of becoming involved
once more with her. That was one line in the sand
he did not cross…. *Unlike virginity, Alex?*

'Does the child's father mind her being brought
up by another man?'

'Would you?' she countered.

He thought about it—but not for long as it was
a no-brainer. 'Yes, I would.' Little Lizzie—not
so little these days—had spent the first few years
of her life farmed out to relatives and friends
before her father had claimed her and given her
the home that had always been hers by rights. To
allow that to happen to a child of his…?

It would never happen! His child would not
suffer an identity crisis. She would always know
where she belonged, she would always feel safe,
loved and secure.

The instant response sent a flurry of panic
through Angel. She brought her lashes down in

a concealing sweep to hide her response. Exhaling a slow, measured, calming breath, she told herself there was no way he could know—and he didn't.

She looked up. There was no shocked realisation, not even a shade of suspicion in his bright eyes.

'I am bringing my daughter up alone.'

'So you make the calls and your boyfriend of the moment acts as a childminder, providing he has no problem with your work taking you away from your family?' It amazed him that any man trusted her enough to let her out of his sight, let alone halfway across the globe.

An energising rush of anger surged through her body as, with lush lips compressed in an angry rose-tinted line, she retorted, 'I would never ever farm my daughter out!'

'Why do you constantly assume I'm judging you?'

'And you're not?' she flung back.

'Or do you judge yourself?' he speculated.

'And for the record there's nothing wrong with a man being the carer.'

He arched a brow. 'Did I say there was?'

'You implied it,' she contended. '*If* I had a boy-friend who wanted to stay at home and look after Jas I'd consider myself lucky.' But she'd refuse. Angel would never allow her child to become fond of someone who could vanish. 'And I don't enjoy being away from Jas.' She swallowed, her voice thickening with emotion she couldn't hide as she added, 'But it won't always be this way. I've given myself five years to make enough to start my own—' She stopped and thought, *You are telling him this why, Angel?*

Out of this information one detail jumped out at Alex. '*If...* You do not have a boyfriend?'

'Why? Are you thinking of applying for the vacancy?' As jokes went this one fell pretty flat. Did the man even have a sense of humour? 'That was a joke. My brother is good at helping out with Jas.'

'You have a brother?'

'We share...' She paused and lowered her gaze from his interrogative stare. She felt disinclined to explain the circumstances that had led her to be living in a wing of the highland castle that her brother had inherited. She had tried to replicate for her daughter the idyllic childhood there that had been snatched away from her and Angel was not about to let anyone tear it away from Jasmine.

'He was available to take care of Jasmine.'

She took a step away from him towards the rocks, taking care to avoid the tideline of broken shells and seaweed that was coarse underfoot. 'Look, I'd better be getting back.'

'Not that way.'

She looked at the hand on her arm, feeling a worrying disinclination to break the contact.

'You can't get back along the beach at high tide.' His hand fell away, leaving Angel conscious of the tingling imprint. 'It is nearly high tide.'

Absently rubbing the spot where his fingers had been, she fought another tide—this time one of rising dismay. Alone on a beach she could have coped—she was resourceful and it appealed to her spirit of adventure—but she wasn't alone!

'We're trapped?'

'Another instalment in your dramatic life.' For a split second he was tempted to say they were trapped, but he stifled the impulse. 'Relax, there's a path through the trees.' He pointed to the pines that lined the beach. 'Slightly longer, but quite well marked. Come on, I'll show you.'

Side by side but not touching, they walked towards the tree-shaded area. The pine needles underfoot crunched as they walked beneath the fragrant canopy. In the softer light the bruise on her forehead was much more evident.

'I think you've escaped a black eye.'

'It's my shoulder that I'll feel tomorrow.' She rotated her shoulder, feeling the stiffness that was bound to get worse before it got better. Her hand went to her head, which she dismissed with a casual, 'I bruise easily.' She stopped, her eyes widening as she turned to him, and she grimaced as she realised the implications of his comment. 'There's a bruise? You can see it?'

He nodded, picking up the concern in her voice and wondering why she was bothered about something she had previously shrugged off.

'Terrific!' Wincing slightly, she traced the slightly raised outline on her temple with her finger. It was not vanity or the pain that gathered her brows into a worried straight line above her tip-tilted nose, but the prospect of what the women in Make-up would say when they saw her, and the horror would likely not be limited to them. The last thing she needed as the new girl was people questioning her professional attitude.

'It's not *that* bad.'

She slung him a gloomy look and continued to walk. 'It is *that* bad if you have lights and a camera pointed at your face. There's only so much even the best make-up and lighting can disguise.'

And even less could she disguise her growing feeling of confusion around him. Life had been simpler before she'd had any insight into the man who had for six years been the focus of her anger. Not a shiny, perfect hero—although he did have a habit of being in the right place to snatch her from the jaws of, if not death, definitely discomfort—but not, it turned out, a serial seducer. He was a man with a family and a history that had left him with his share of emotional scars and even, it seemed, the odd moral value.

Struggling to lift his eyes from the long, sinuous curves of her sleek brown body, his gaze drawn to the tiny slice of paler skin where her bikini bottom had slipped down over the angle of her hip bone, he shrugged.

'Can they not film around your scenes?'

Angel laughed. She could not imagine that this

would be the response from the team when she appeared looking this way. 'This is an advert, not a blockbuster. I'm in all the scenes and, as they keep telling me, time is money.'

'No, time is a luxury.'

They had reached the point where the trees thinned and the hotel came into view.

'A luxury I don't have.' She expelled a deep sigh. 'Ah, well, I'd better face the music.' She turned to him. 'I might not have said it. In fact, I know I didn't, but thank you for fishing me out of the drink. I really am grateful.'

He looked down at her with an odd expression. 'I do not want your thanks—I want this!'

Without warning, he bent his head and covered her mouth with his. A primitive thrill shot through her and she moaned into his mouth, responding to the hunger of his lips, melting against him as she was carried along on a dizzy tide of raw need. Not fighting it, not questioning, just sinking into all the warm darkness that only he seemed able to tap into and going with it. The relief...the release, it was incredible! She had stopped being the person she tried so hard to be and let herself be the person she was—with him.... *Why him?*

As abruptly as it had begun, it ended.

They stood there staring at each other. Angel saw wariness in his blue eyes then, with a muttered imprecation, he turned away.

She remained where she was, her eyes wide, her hand to her mouth as he stalked away back along the path they had just walked along.

# CHAPTER SIX

AFTER HER FACE had been viewed from all angles and all light conditions by all interested parties, including the dermatologist who had been shipped in when Clive had developed a spot, it was decided that the situation was not as bad as originally feared. In three days' time the swelling would be gone and the bruises that make-up didn't disguise could be airbrushed away.

Three days was not long enough to fly home and see Jas, but long enough to miss her like hell. With nothing to fill her day, Angel found sheer boredom set in very quickly. Sunbathing on a beach might be many people's idea of bliss, but Angel had never been good at sitting still doing nothing.

With no other suggestions after she had been banned from doing anything that might injure her and delay the schedule further, she ended up armed with a pair of knitting needles, a ball of bright blue wool and instructions from Clive, who assured her a child could do it. He predicted she'd be amazed at how relaxing it was so she sat beneath a palm tree and set about being creative.

Half an hour later, her teeth aching with tension, she grabbed the tangled lot and flung it across the beach. She knew she was acting like a spoiled child, if you discounted the adult expletive that accompanied the action. She knew it wasn't the minor frustration that made her want to yell and stamp her feet, it was everything that had gone before and what was to come. Her teeth ached with the tension that was tying her body in knots. Not thinking was exhausting. If she could have rid herself of the decisions she had to make in the same way she had that damned wool—the colour reminded her of his eyes—she might have been able to enjoy a moment's peace.

Before the voice, the prickling on the back of her neck had warned her she wasn't alone. Even so, she flinched when he spoke.

'It's an instant fine for littering here.'

How long had he been watching her?

She turned her head in the direction of the mocking drawl but sat rigidly, watching as he gathered up her rejected knitting and walked back towards her. It was just her luck. Miles of beach and he had to walk along the stretch that she had chosen. Ashamed of the ache of longing that made her throat dry, she followed his progress across the sand.

Alex was in no hurry, but as he got closer her heart rate became more erratic. Pressing a hand to her chest, she lowered her gaze and trained her eyes on his bare feet. It seemed a relatively safe part of his anatomy to focus on until, unable to stop herself, she lifted her gaze up over his hair-roughened calves and muscular thighs. The khaki shorts he wore were belted low over his narrow hips and his short-sleeved shirt hung open, revealing his lean ribbed brown torso.

'So are you here to arrest me?' She extended her hands, wrists crossed for imaginary cuffs. 'I'll come quietly.'

'Now that I find hard to believe.' The idea of her giving up without a fight brought a grim smile to his face as he dropped her knitting needles onto her lap. 'Actually I'm here to save you.'

The comment drew a sardonic laugh from Angel. The only thing she needed saving from was standing right there, sending her entire nervous system into a state of chaos, with his long, greyhound-lean limbs, oozing sex from every perfect pore.

'From death by boredom.'

'Who says I'm bored?'

He reached down and picked off a fibre of bright blue wool that clung to his shorts. He arched a sardonic brow and let the fibre blow away. 'You're bored.' And unless he was totally out in his assessment, as eaten up with burning frustration as he was.

Bored...much worse, thought Angel. She was hopelessly aroused—just looking at him made her nerve endings tingle. She pressed a hand across her middle to ease the heavy dragging sensation low in her pelvis. There was no place to hide except behind the big floppy hat she wore and the sunglasses that hid her eyes from him.

She produced a scowl. 'Isn't that littering or are you a special case?'

His white teeth flashed. 'I like to think so.'

She stroked a restless hand up and down her smooth calf. 'I'm not good at sitting still.' Catching the direction of his gaze, she stopped stroking and pushed her sunglasses back up on her nose.

The admission did not come as a surprise. She was not exactly what could be termed a restful woman: stubborn, aggressive, confrontational… As he mentally made a list of her less desirable qualities his eyes followed her hand to her face. All that was visible was her firm, rounded chin and her mouth, and there was nothing at all restful about those plump, luscious lips. An unfocused glaze drifted into his eyes as he struggled and failed to suppress the memory of those lips parting beneath his.

The silence stretched and he stood there looming over her like a statue until she could bear it no more.

'I think you're the one that's bored.' She aimed for cool and haughty but achieved something more akin to sulky.

In response he flopped down on the sand beside her, intensifying her cowardly impulse to run. His shoulder was an inch from hers. If she could have figured out a way of widening that gap without being obvious she would have.

Maybe what people said was right: that you

could run but you couldn't hide...? On the other hand you could try, at least when it came to examining your own feelings.

Angel jammed the tangled mess from her lap into the massive holdall, managing to jab one of the needles into her leg. 'Ouch!'

'Been for a swim?' He could see the outline of her bikini under the thin thigh-length cover-up she wore.

'I'm not allowed. In fact I'm banned from pretty much everything apart from breathing and I'm in everybody's bad books.'

'They can't blame you for saving a kid's life.'

'Why not?' she countered. 'You did...and saving his life is a bit of an exaggeration.' She jammed her unread paperback on top of the knitting and clicked the clasp of the big raffia bag closed.

'Ever modest.' And ever a temptation. He stared at her mouth, wanting to slide his tongue between those beautiful, provocative lips. The need was so strong that for the space of several heartbeats he lost track of his real objective.

She sniffed and pushed her sunglasses up the bridge of her nose, flashing a small, tense smile.

'That's me…it's just a shame I'm not the creative type.' She nodded at the bag.

He adopted an expression of innocent surprise. 'Really? I thought you went to art school.'

'I didn't finish the course—' Her expression tensed as she flashed a suspicious look his way. 'How did you know that?' she demanded, whisking her knees up to her chin and wrapping her arms protectively around her calves.

He shrugged casually. 'Someone must have mentioned it.'

Or something, namely the bio in the short report provided by the people who normally did background checks on prospective employees for him, a report that concerned specifically the months prior to the birth of Angelina Urquart's daughter…and most importantly that date.

It had been 3:00 a.m. when the seed of the idea had first entered his head. It had spent the next hour insidiously burrowing in, taking root while he had spent that period by turns becoming totally convinced he was right and equally totally convinced that the idea was a combined product of his overactive imagination, sexual frustration and sleep deprivation.

He needed to know—he needed to know at what point a nightmare became a premonition and for that he needed information. Alex had not bothered to work out time differences. He would not have used a firm who were not available on a twenty-four-hour basis and the person whose direct line he rang sounded alert and helpful—he expected nothing less.

They could not supply the information he really desired, but what they could supply and did was information that could confirm that it was possible.

The details that popped into his email box at 5:00 a.m. gave the bare facts he had requested: Angelina Urquart had given birth to a daughter eight months to the day after they had spent the night together.

He could be a father. Statistically speaking it was probable he was guilty of the crime that he had found it so easy to condemn his father for.

That it was possible to have a child, be a father and not know... He could have walked past his own daughter in the street and not guessed who she was. The idea utterly appalled him, but did fatherhood?

Running normally cleared his head. Facing the idea of being a father while covered in sweat and breathing hard, it still remained totally shocking but not the nightmare he had expected it to be. Was he feeling what his own father had the day that Lizzie's aunt had turned up with the child and a stack of letters that the child's dead mother had written but never sent, to dramatically inform the stunned man in front of a room full of party guests that it was his turn now to take responsibility for the child he had fathered?

At least he had some privacy to get his head around the concept and his big reveal would be at a time and place of his own choosing…if there was a reveal. After all, the question mark remained.

If he was right, why hadn't Angel told him? Did she ever plan to tell him? As he felt his anger mount the sense of loss he experienced, thinking of the years he had missed and would never get back, made it tough to see the situation from her point of view…but he was trying.

She came across as confident, but how much of that was window dressing? Six years younger, alone and presumably scared out of her wits at finding herself pregnant, had she tried to find him? Thoughts of her in that state of mind increased the guilt that gnawed away at him like acid. On one level he recognised that she wouldn't have known where to start to look for him, and in that case he knew that she hadn't set out to deprive him of parenthood. But on another level, he wondered if she hadn't been secretly relieved. Her opinion of him was so bad that she probably thought he would make a catastrophic parent.

His jaw clenched. For a man who rarely found himself not in a position of control to be forced to recognise that his position as an unmarried father gave him precious few rights, let alone control, was tough for Alex.

He was going to be part of his child's life no matter what it took.... The thought of another man thinking access to Angel's bed gave him the right to become a father to her child was a situation that he could not contemplate.

'So why didn't you complete your course?'

The question was casual but something in the way he was looking at her made her uneasy. Angel dodged his gaze and shrugged. Maybe she was getting paranoid but Angel responded to the alarm bells. 'I had some distractions.'

A baby.

His baby?

It had been several hours now since he had faced the possibility; the emotional impact had felt like a ten-tonne truck landing on his chest. Three hours to run, pace, speculate and plan…the weight remained but his brain was now clearer. The solution was there and he would do whatever it took to get the information.

Information that was stored in one place—her beautiful little head.

Not for nothing had the business world named him the perfect poker player. There were no 'tells' to even hint at an agenda behind his casual invitation. 'And how about now?'

She shook her head and gave a shrug of incomprehension.

'Could you do with some distraction?'

She clamped her lips tight over an outraged gasp. 'Well, no one could accuse you of subtlety, could they? Thanks for the offer but no, thanks.'

He gave a throaty laugh. 'Actually I wasn't propositioning you. Don't be embarrassed.'

She stuck her chin out. Embarrassed did not cover the toe-curling mortification that made her want to literally bury her head in the sand. Anything was preferable to seeing his smug face. 'This,' she gritted, circling her face with a finger, 'is relief.'

He took her chin between his thumb and forefinger and with the other hand pushed her shades up into her hair. The action was casual, confident, as though he had the right to touch her. *You're not doing much to disabuse him of this massive misapprehension, are you, Angel, just sitting there like some sort of mesmerised rabbit?* she thought to herself. When she ought to be... What...?

'No, this is beautiful....' he husked.

Trying to kick-start her brain felt like wading through warm syrup. *This is not me.... Why does he make me act this way? Why do I let him do this to me?*

*Because you like it?*

The crazy thought almost made her laugh. She pulled her sunglasses down again.

'I'd love to discuss your idea but—'

Angel dug her fingernails into her palms, focusing on the pain to help her fight her way to control. She turned her head and his hand fell away.

Digging her heels into the sand, she said, 'It wasn't an idea.' Her voice sounded very small, the scornful laugh weak— Well, actually, pathetically unconvincing.

'Don't sulk,' he said, drawing an outraged gasp. 'Obviously I want to have sex with you.'

He delivered this piece of information in a manner she associated more with ordering a pizza than propositioning. The violent lurch in her chest was possibly, Angel mused, her heart stopping. Despite the possibility of her imminent expiration she somehow—it was a miracle—kept her expression blank. Thank goodness for sunglasses.

'I get that a lot.'

Not a lie, but she'd never felt in danger of requiring CPR before. Or...best to treat the comment as a joke—the alternative was not something she felt equipped to cope with.

She saw something flash in his eyes—anger?

'I'm sure you do,' he countered smoothly, 'but

on this occasion I was thinking more along the lines of lunch.'

Lunch with Alex Arlov? Now, that was a crazy idea.

Or was it? Wasn't this an opportunity to get to know Jas's father in the nonbiblical sense? She still needed to decide if he was a man she wanted to be involved in her daughter's life. For that judgement she had to put her personal feelings aside.

And what were her personal feelings?

She gave her head a tiny shake and pulled her hat more firmly down on her dark hair, glad that he could not hear her thoughts or, thanks to the tinted lenses, see her confusion. Normally someone who had a head-on approach to life, she had been skirting around that question since he had reappeared in her life.

And with good reason. Feelings... It sounded so simple but how was she meant to analyse something so, so...*visceral*? It was easier to accept it. What was the point of delving deeper? At its most basic, she was attracted to him, but that hardly made her special. She had seen the way women looked at him...all women. He was a man who inspired lust and around him she dropped several IQ points; her brain just didn't function at full capacity. In fact sometimes it just didn't function full stop!

Well, they were welcome to him, she told herself. At least she had the maturity now to be able to differentiate between lust and deeper, more profound emotions.

*Tell that to your nervous system!*

'Eating is not one of the things you are barred from doing, is it?' He unscrewed the bottle of water he had been carrying. Halfway to his mouth he paused and extended it towards her. 'Want some?'

'No, thank you,' she responded, primly polite.

'Is it?' he said, wiping his mouth with his hand.

She started guiltily—her eyes had been riveted on the muscles working in his brown throat as he swallowed. 'What?'

'They haven't banned you from eating?'

'That depends on the calorie count. They are worried about my hips.' She was regretting the flippant remark even before she had finished speaking, but managed not to make the moment any worse by successfully resisting the impulse to tug the spangled, jewel-bright fabric of her cover-up lower over her hips. As his head tilted to one side his eyes slid over her sleek, smooth curves, lingering on the supposed problem area.

After a nerve-shredding moment his gaze lifted, his expression blank, but the glow in his eyes made her stomach flip. 'Yes, I can see you must need to be careful,' he delivered in a dead-pan tone, thinking that he had never met a woman who so totally encapsulated all things erotic and sensual.

Wide and indignant, her eyes flew to his face. A moment later her tension fell away and she was laughing in response to the gleam in his blue eyes. Then the gleam changed, became not amused, and she looked away quickly, her heart thudding, her mouth dry.

'How would you like it if I drew attention to your flaws?' He didn't have any—at least not physical ones.

'You brought your hips into this discussion,' he reminded her. 'Not that I'm complaining, and if you're going to tell me you have any self-esteem issues don't waste your breath.'

His heavy-lidded glance moved from her lips,

sweeping downwards over the length of her sinuous, sleek, leggy frame. No woman could be as
unselfconscious in bed as Angel had been if she
was not happy in her own skin. She had taken
pleasure from her own body as much as she had
from his, and he had never known a woman to
display such fascination with his body before or
since.

Without warning a piercing stab of pure lust
sliced through him, raising the level of his arousal
painfully as he allowed the door in his head to
open a crack for the memories to push through,
not in a controlled way but in one hot, steamy
rush. His brilliant eyes darkened and glazed with
licking flames as he saw…felt…her hands gliding over his skin, the moisture of her tongue.

Her lovemaking had been as generous as her
cushiony soft lips… It had never crossed his mind
for a split second that she had been a virgin, not
even when she had been so tight when he had
entered. There had been that shocked little cry,
but he had taken that as a compliment.

*Maybe you didn't want to know, Alex?*

The sudden audible crack of his finger joints
made Angel's questioning gaze shift from his ex-

tended fingers to his face. The golden skin was pulled taut across his magnificent bones; his angular jaw was tensed; his eyes remained hidden by the luxuriant sweep of his preposterously long eyelashes.

She could see the tension in the rigidity of his powerful shoulders as he reached down and took her hand.

'You shouldn't be sitting here in the midday sun.'

She didn't react to his impatient tone; she reacted to an unacknowledged desire to make contact and to the fizz of electricity through her body that made her head buzz as she allowed him to pull her to her feet.

When she pulled her fingers free they continued to tingle. She held her hand against her chest and struggled to take control of her breathing... and then found she was virtually panting! Acting like some sort of sexually deprived bimbo was sending out all the wrong messages.

Or, more worryingly, the right ones!

Her laughter was as uninhibited as her lovemaking had been in his thoughts.

'I will personally guarantee your physical

safety.' He arched a brow and held out a hand towards her. 'I have said something that amuses you?'

She looked at the hand and thought, *You don't make me feel safe. A lot of other things, but not safe.*

'I don't require a bodyguard.'

Their glances connected and suddenly the fizz between them made it hard for her to breathe.

'How about a charming companion and lunch?'

'Really?' She made a pantomime of looking around. 'Where would I find one of those?' she asked, before adding almost shyly, 'Lunch would be good.'

When her desperate attempt at humour did not produce even a half smile Angel huffed a sigh. 'I am hungry,' she admitted, thinking, *Where is the harm?* And she was doing this for Jas. She wasn't looking for a soulmate, but that was no reason to deprive her daughter of a dad. Though that did depend on the dad…. And how was she meant to judge if he was good enough for Jas if she ran away every time she saw him?

What sort of man was he?

Oh, she'd read the stuff on the internet and

knew about the wealth, the enigmatic reputation that had resulted in some wild speculation, and she took all that with a pinch of salt, but the man did come across as a mass of contradictions.

They walked in silence along the path that led from the beach through sweet-scented pine trees. Once or twice she looked up at the tall man walking beside her and he seemed lost in thought and showed no inclination to engage her in conversation. This suited Angel, who made no attempt to break the stalemate, though, as she mockingly told herself, in order to get to know him she might have to speak at some point.

As they reached the place where the path entered the hotel's gardens Alex took a left turn instead and opened a gate marked Private that had always previously been locked.

'Where are we going?' She had her answer as they rounded the bend and a small cove came into view. It was empty but for the motor launch moored off the rocks.

'For lunch. Careful, the rocks are slippery.'

'I thought we were going to the hotel.'

'We're not.' He did not elaborate.

'I can see that,' she returned, ignoring his hand.

She was making a point, a trivial one perhaps, but it felt important to emphasise the fact that she could cope alone. Or was she simply prepared to fall rather than risk experiencing the electrical surge that occurred whenever she touched him?

With a frown she pushed the intrusive suggestion away and, with one hand out to balance, the other holding the heavy swathe of her hair out of her eyes, she inched her way cautiously down the rocks, aware that landing on her bottom would prove both painful and humiliating.

Her refusal to accept a helping hand, literally, brought a small ironic twist to his lips. The action encapsulated the woman: stubborn, reckless and damned irritating. But he conceded as he watched her from the vantage point of the boat that she really was the most incredibly graceful and alluring creature he had ever seen.

There were very few people who could make slipping and slithering look elegant, but she was one of them. His jaw clenched as he restrained himself from flying to her rescue after a particularly spectacular lurch.... If she fell and broke her beautiful neck it would serve her right.

This was no path, thought Angel, more a free

climb, and the appeal of clinging to a rock face with nothing to harness you for pleasure passed Angel by. She decided it was a case of practicality over pride, but a few feet from the end of the rocky path she did not refuse the hand he reached out. She'd made her point and it was quite a leap into the boat.

He had made it look easy, of course.

'Thank you.'

His ironic grin broadened as he clasped her hand, then vanished as she landed. The momentum of her landing sent her crashing into his body and the flash of heat that slid down his front caused his smile to fade. His heavy eyelids lowered, hiding the hard, hungry look in them, as his hands on her elbows pushed her away and he directed a cool, 'Steady!' to the top of her head.

Concealing the fact that all his instincts were telling him to grab that gorgeous behind and mould her to him came at a price, in the form of the pain in his groin and the slick of sweat that lay like a fine sheen over the surface of his skin. Despite appearances and the Northern blood running in his veins, he was immune to the heat, but the same could not be said of a soft warm female, at least not when it came in the dangerous form of Angel Urquart.

'We're eating on Saronia?' she speculated, experiencing mixed feelings about this journey into the unknown. The caution was sensible, the excitement was not!

'Don't you like surprises?'

'Only some of them.'

'Come on, Angel,' he urged, mocking her with his electric-blue eyes. 'Live dangerously.'

Angel looked away, remembering what had happened the last time she had lived dangerously. Now she was a mother who was going to provide her daughter with what she had craved as a child: a calm, nurturing environment to grow up in. Combustible relationships were not on the agenda and there was no escaping the fact that sparks flew every time she came within the same square mile as Alex.

Unlike yesterday, she was in a position to actually appreciate the wind-in-your-face experience of cutting through the water in the fast speedboat. She sat back, knowing the journey would not last long, though it turned out to be a little longer than she anticipated. Instead of mooring where the film crew were dropped off, he continued on, following the coastline.

The filming had all taken place at the side of the island that faced the mainland. They had been requested not to leave the immediate area so she had never seen this side of the island, and she immediately saw how different it was—much greener and more lush.

He cut the engine and brought the boat expertly up to the edge of the small wooden pier.

'There used to be a road from the other side of the island but it fell into disrepair. The only access now is by water or helipad.'

It turned out there was no road this side either. The stony, near-vertical route he drove the open-topped four-wheel drive along barely deserved to be called a track. Halfway up the hill Angel, who was hanging onto the overhead strap, turned her head and yelled, 'If you're going to drive like this, you might at least put two hands on the steering wheel.'

He threw her a lazy smile. 'You're a back-seat driver.'

Angel didn't respond. They had just topped the crest of the hill and she was staring at the scene revealed in front of her. The pristine sand was as silver white as the Hebrides, the long waving grass behind it dotted with wild flowers, and set in the middle of the green rippling carpet was a white marquee and pitched under it was set a long table. Two figures were unloading items from the four-wheel drive vehicle parked close by.

'If I'd known I would have dressed.'

She half expected the couple who were unloading food to wait on them, but they drove away after a quick word with Alex. As she watched them vanish and responded to the light touch between her shoulder blades that made her conscious of every prickling inch of her skin she realised just how alone they were.

She gave a laugh to cover her nerves and approached the shaded table covered with a white cloth laid with silver and crystal.

'This is your idea of a picnic?' It might be some people's idea of a seduction scene. Discounting the possibility and the flip of excitement low in her pelvis, she was sure that he wouldn't have gone to this much trouble for nothing. The question remained—a lot of effort, but why?

'I don't like sand in my food.'

'You could always concrete over the beach.'

'An idea, but I have to think about my eco credentials.'

'Especially as they're so profitable.'

The muttered response drew a thin smile from him. 'You are, as always, eager to assign the worst possible motives to my actions.'

She opened her mouth to deny this charge and closed it again, her eyes sliding from his as she mumbled, 'I can be a cynic.'

'If you're interested in all things eco you might like to look around my house sometime.'

Following the direction of his gesture, she frowned, seeing only a grassy hill above the high-tide mark, but then a glint of light reflected off glass caught her attention.

'Goodness!'

'Yes, it's easy to miss at first, isn't it?' The architects had fulfilled their brief and made the structure blend in with the landscape, but they had gone one step further—they had made it part of the landscape.

Excavated into the hillside, his sanctuary with its turf roof and no manufactured walls was invisible from most angles, but the clever design meant that every room was flooded with light from the massive glass panels that faced the sea.

'You live there?' It was not the power statement that she had assumed any home of his would be.

'I stay there occasionally. It suits my needs, but it is not equipped for entertaining, hence...' He gestured to the table.

'Won't you sit down?' He pulled out one of the chairs and, feeling both awkward and anxious, she took her seat.

The first fifteen minutes did not give her any insight into him as a person. His conversational skills were as she had expected but he managed to avoid any personal questions, instead turning them back on her. It was deeply frustrating.

'You do not care for seafood?'

Angel, who had been pushing her food around her plate, set her fork down and decided the best approach was a direct one.

'Why did you ask me here? Not to talk about the food, I'm sure.' Nibbling on her lower lip, she caught hold of one of the crystals that weighed down the cloth, rolling it between her fingers.

'Why did you come?' he countered.

She set her elbows on the table and stared

across at him. 'Do you always respond to a question with another question?'

His brows knitted as he forked a large prawn into his mouth. 'I am resisting the temptation to say pot, kettle, black.'

'Not very well,' she inserted sourly.

'The answer to your question is, yes, I do, when the answer interests me.'

'I was bored and hungry.'

'You haven't eaten much.'

'I'm watching my weight.'

'Do you ever worry about your part in the message that the media sends out to young girls?' His tone was deceptively casual but the eyes that met hers were anything but.

'Message?'

'The pressure to achieve an impossible level of perfection, like the women they see in the magazines. The message that equates beauty with happiness. Of course, I was forgetting you have a daughter of your own. I'm sure you are well aware of the pressures facing young women.'

She stiffened, her heart beating fast as she twisted the linen napkin between her fingers.

He knew, somehow he knew! Or he thought he knew….

'Jasmine is not a woman. She's a child.'

'True, but they grow up so quickly and I believe that anorexia sufferers are getting younger and younger.'

She shook her head, angry now, and got to her feet. Looking down at him lessened the feeling of being a mouse being toyed with by a large feline. 'Why are you suddenly so interested in my daughter?'

He laid his own napkin down with slow deliberation, holding her eyes as he got to his feet. 'Because I had this idea… It's crazy, but in my experience those are the ones that it pays not to ignore. So I did a little research and a few surprising things came up, like the fact that your daughter was born eight months to the day after we spent the night together and there was no one before.'

'Or after.' *Did I really say that?*

He didn't react, but she could feel the emotions rolling off him.

Angel didn't blink; she didn't breathe. She

shrugged and struggled to hold on to her manufactured calm.

'So you want to know if you're Jasmine's father? Couldn't you just have come out and asked?
Did it really require all this elaborate stage-
managing?'

'It occurred to me that you might be waiting
for the right moment to tell me…?' He had really
tried hard to think of this from her point of view
but her expression was not saying she appreciated
the effort. He had been her only lover.… Only…
He experienced a stab of sheer primitive possessive satisfaction, and breathed out, letting the air
escape in a slow, measured sigh.

'I thought I'd provide it.… I thought if you
were relaxed—'

'You thought you'd get me drunk,' she countered, pointing to the second bottle in the ice
bucket. 'And trick me into saying things!'

The comment hit a raw nerve. First she threw
his consideration back in his face, now she tried
to make herself the victim. 'I shouldn't have to
trick you into anything. If I've got a bloody child
I have a right to know.… I have a right to know
her!' It was the first time she had heard him use

Russian but she was guessing she wouldn't find the translation of what he snarled in any phrase book.

As angry now as he was, she heaved in a taut, angry breath of her own. What did he know? Parenthood wasn't a right—it was a privilege!

'Rights? You have no rights! You see Jasmine only if I say so, and I don't. I came here wanting to find out if you were the sort of person I want in Jasmine's life, the sort of person who would be good for her to know. Well, now I do know, and you're not. I wouldn't have you near my daughter…for…for…anything! You're a manipulative bastard who treats people like chess pieces… You're the last father I'd choose for my daughter.'

Breathing hard like duelists, they stood either end of the table facing one another, firing angry words, not bullets, though the words could inflict considerable damage and once they were out there they were impossible to retract.

Even though she was still furious Angel was already beginning to regret the things she had said.

He leaned forward, his hands flat on the table, and fixed her with an icy blue arctic stare. When he spoke it was in a voice that was several deci-bels lower than the hot words shouted in the heat of the moment. Cold, considered and chosen to inflict the maximum level of fear.

Angel was seeing the man that made powerful men tremble with fear.

'You have picked the wrong man to challenge. You will not keep my daughter from me. At-tempt to prevent me seeing her and it will be me you come begging to for visitation rights. If you have a skeleton… If you have a bone fragment in your cupboard I will find it and my lawyers will use it.' He hardened his heart against her pale, stricken expression and added, 'You started this, but I will finish it. That much is a promise.'

Without another word he walked away.

Angel didn't react. She just stood there, fro-zen. She roused only at the sound of an engine and she turned in time to see him vanishing in a cloud of dust.

He had driven away, leaving her stranded.

Not quite able to believe the situation she found herself in, she looked from the dust cloud to the food and wine spread out and with a laugh she slumped down into the chair.

'At least I won't starve.'

She was still sitting there twenty minutes later when one of the men who had earlier been laying out the food appeared. If he found the situation strange nothing in his manner suggested it as he framed his meticulously polite question.

'Are you ready to return to the mainland?'

She was ready to kiss the feet of her rescuer but she was much more circumspect in her icy state, and responded to the respectful enquiry with a nod and a smile.

# CHAPTER SEVEN

ALEX PULLED THE car over after a mile, leaning his elbows across the steering wheel. He thought he knew every inch of the island but he struggled to get his bearings as he pushed his head back into the padded headrest and looked up through the open roof at the trees that blocked out the sun.

'Well, that worked out well, Alex.'

He'd had it all planned. While he had rejected all Angel's charges at the time, had she been so wrong?

Driving like a lunatic, while satisfying, was not going to solve anything. He had blown it; he had acted while the emotive impact of discovering he was a father was still fresh. When she hadn't said what he'd wanted to hear he had launched into attack mode and made a tough situation ten times worse.

Back at the bungalow the only thing she wanted to do was... Actually there were two things she wanted to do: throw herself on the bed and weep, and break something. The first she didn't do because she was due to have her prearranged chat via the internet with her daughter in less than half an hour, and the second... Well, she was supposedly a grown-up and grown-ups did not throw their rattles out of the pram, unless of course the supposed grown-up was Alex Arlov!

Things hadn't gone his way and he'd simply gone off in a strop. Admittedly, a pretty magnificently broody strop, but the fact remained that she had refused to play by his rules so he'd walked away, issuing threats that had made her blood turn to ice. Not to mention that they revealed what a truly ruthless man lurked beneath the urbane exterior.

Would he adopt the same sort of parenting style? When the going got tough would he opt out?

Her hands balled into clawed fists at her side as she paced the room. The man made her so mad! She took a deep breath and reminded herself that this was not about her or her feelings, or, for that matter, Alex. It was about Jas and she was not going to run the risk of laying her precious girl open to hurt or rejection.

It was after her chat with Jas that Angel did cry—tears of regret more than anger. Her little girl was so lovely. She deserved a father, someone who would take her as she was, and not weigh her down with unrealistic expectations. Did Alex even know what having a child involved? Or would Jas just be another possession to him?

Had he meant those threats?

Should she get legal advice? The thought of anyone trying to take away her daughter... She shuddered as she recalled his lethally soft-voiced threat, aimed with dagger-like accuracy to inflict the maximum fear and panic.

She wouldn't panic; she would fight!

The last thing she felt like later that evening was being sociable, but Angel knew that her no-show would be construed as standoffishness by the others so she was forced to sit around the big table and smile her way through the evening. She responded good-naturedly to the teasing about her heroics until she realised why the ad-agency man who had been the most vocal in his exasperation after the resulting delay now seemed quite jovial about the subject.

She expressed her relief to Clive, who was sitting beside her. 'I'm glad he's calmed down.'

'Of course he's calmed down, darling—all that free publicity!'

Angel shook her head. 'Publicity?'

'Seriously?' The slightly tipsy Hollywood actor scanned her face for signs of irony, then, finding none, laughed hilariously, causing someone at the opposite end of the table to request being let into the joke.

'It turns out that our Angel is one of life's innocents. She doesn't know that someone recorded the whole hero thing on their phone and uploaded it onto the web.' He turned back to Angel and explained with a touch of envy he didn't quite disguise, 'You have gone viral. All that free publicity is better than sex as far as our Jake is concerned, and the only thing the world loves more than a heroine is a heroine that looks like you do in a bikini.'

The other man raised a glass at the charge.

'Oh, God, no!'

Her genuine horror made Carl laugh even more. 'Of course, there are some theories the whole thing was staged. Don't you just love conspiracy theories?'

'No.' She huffed out an exasperated sigh. Clive's blend of superficial charm and malicious humour was beginning to pall. Compared to Alex's far more abrasive, abrupt and in your face— God, why was she even thinking about Alex, let alone using him as a measure of male perfection? She couldn't think of anything less perfect. She closed down the inner dialogue with a resounding snap and produced a clear, focused smile. Nobody could accuse her of being obsessed. 'I don't, but I believe in respecting a person's right to privacy.'

The actor gave a shaky smile, clearly in two minds. Was she being serious…? 'Ever thought you were in the wrong line of work, darling?'

'Frequently,' she admitted, permitting herself a dry laugh before she turned her attention to Sandy on her right. Her present career was a means to an end, something she had fallen into rather than planned. She had given herself five years, and if at that point she had not made enough money to set herself up with the fashion-design label she had mapped out in her head then she would walk away with no regrets and possibly more than a little relief.

Angel made it through the meal, avoided the copious free-flowing wine, but not even her sweet tooth gave her the appetite to make it through the pudding course. Pleading tiredness, which was not a lie, she made her excuses early and during her walk back to her bungalow found fifty messages when it occurred to her to check her phone!

She only replied to the two from her brother. It took even longer than she had anticipated to calm and reassure him, and she agreed with his decision not to keep Jas up to speed with her mother's newfound fame. In the back of her mind she wondered if being an internet heroine would be a plus or a minus if the fight got to court?

Her brother hadn't laid a guilt trip on her; it wasn't his style. But even so, Angel was feeling pretty much a failure as a mother by the time she reached her bungalow and searched for the swipe card for the door.

'It's not locked. Anyone could have walked in.'

Angel yelped and spun around as the tall figure emerged from the shadows. Even without the moonlight that illuminated his face, revealing the strong sybaritic slashing angles and spine-tinglingly strong bones, it would have been impossible to mistake the identity of the person who was lurking there.

'And did you?' She managed to project a level of cool she knew she didn't have a hope of sustaining for long. The sound of his voice had begun a chain reaction that she had no control over; his physical presence made the feelings that were surging unchecked through her body even more urgent and mortifyingly obvious.

How could you hate someone and want them at the same time?

She crossed a hand over her chest, unable to restrain a wince when it brushed the shamelessly engorged nipples she was attempting to hide. Her heart was in her throat, the dull, thunderous clamour echoing in her ears drowning out the more peaceful sound of the waves as she lifted her chin to an imperious angle and repeated her accusation.

'Well, did you?'

'I thought I'd wait to be invited.'

'Then you'll have a hell of a long wait.' A predictable response and, she realised, shamefully untrue. Where this man was concerned, instead of locking doors she had a terrible tendency to fling them wide open and drag him in!

He didn't react to the belligerent challenge. Instead his narrowed eyes followed the hand she wiped across her face. 'You're shaking.'

Acutely conscious of the unblinking blue stare, she responded to the note of accusation in his voice with a resentful, 'Probably because the last person who jumped out from behind a bush as I was trying to open my door now has a restraining order against him.'

The mocking smile vanished from his face. 'A restraining order?' A relationship turned sour, violent...? His hand clenched. 'Who was... Is this man?'

Angel, already regretting she had mentioned the incident, shrugged. 'Just a sad man. He was harmless really.'

A nerve clenched in his cheek as Alex stared at her in stunned disbelief. She sounded so calm, so casual!

'So harmless you took out a restraining order against him.' His sardonic statement was shot through with audible anger, the same anger that made his blue eyes burn as he focused on it instead of the sick lurch in the pit of his belly as he imagined her defenceless, vulnerable and at the mercy of some crazed lunatic. Yet today he had ripped into her himself, issuing every kind of threat he could think of…trying to hurt her.

'It turned out all he was carrying was a bracelet.'

'What did you think he was carrying?'

'A knife,' she admitted, adding with an embarrassed grimace, 'What can I say? I watch too many cop shows on telly.'

'You thought I was a knife-wielding maniac?'

She moved her head in a negative motion. 'You surprised me, that's all. And he didn't have a knife and he wasn't really a maniac, though obviously not entirely right in the head.' She accompanied the explanation with an illustrative tap on her own head, thinking as she did so that perhaps she was in no position to throw stones.

After all, sane did not exactly describe her own reaction when she had seen him as being that of someone in full possession of all her mental faculties. Her stomach muscles were still quivering.

She had spent the best part of the evening calling him every name under the sun, inside her head of course, but the moment she had seen him her throat had thickened and her traitorous heart had started to thud.

'A person who serves you coffee and decides your smile means you are soulmates has issues. Obviously if I'd realised it was just another of his presents I wouldn't have hit him over the head with the plant pot, though maybe it was a good thing I did,' she mused. 'Because the plant pot actually proved a lot more effective than a police warning and he decided that I was not his soul-mate after all.'

'Plant pot?' he echoed, struggling to wade through this information.

'It was the only thing there.'

The note of apology drew a choked sound from his throat and he realised it was impossible to judge Angel by the other women he knew. She was clearly a creature who acted on instinct.

Combine that sort of reckless impetuosity with youth and a passionate nature and it wasn't hard to see how she had ended up pregnant. But then the mystery was how he had been the first. He still struggled to get his head around that knowledge.

Alex had no excuse, which was why he was here and he couldn't allow himself to be distracted.

'The things you said this afternoon... You were right. You were not telling me anything I don't already know.... I just wasn't ready to hear it.' She watched as he dragged his hand through his dark hair, which, she noticed, was already tousled. He was still wearing the same clothes he had been in earlier that day, though they were a lot more creased, and for the first time since that night six years ago she was seeing his jaw shadowed with dark stubble.

'From me?' She anticipated a savage rebuttal and got instead a thoroughly and totally disarming tip of his head.

'This is your call and I will abide by your decision. The threats I made were...selfish. I'm sorry, you were right. You have every reason to hate me. I slept with you, I took no precautions, it was thoughtless, I've never...' He just stopped himself producing the classic 'I've never done it before' line. After all, why should she believe it?

Actions, he reminded himself, spoke louder than words. 'I want to make things right.'

Angel was shaken by the depth of self-loathing in his voice, but she forced a laugh and framed her ironic rebuttal in a voice as cold as she could make it. 'You want Jasmine.'

The goad made the lines bracketing his mouth tighten but he managed to hide his frustration, well aware that once already today he had barged in like the proverbial china-shop bull, issuing threats when he should have been asking questions, building bridges.

'It's true, I want to be a father to my child. But you were right—I'm in no position to call the shots.'

Not being in a position to call the shots, as he termed it, had to be a new experience for him. But Angel was not totally trusting of this new Alex, and she refused to be lulled into a false sense of security. She would not lower her defences just yet.

'That's a pretty big U-turn for someone who was talking custody battles not a few hours ago.'

'I told you about Lizzie…'

'Your half-sister?'

He nodded. 'She was ten before she knew who her father was, before she knew *she* was wanted.... I want Jasmine to know she is wanted.'

The soft addition sliced through her determined stance of wary hostility. There was no question of his sincerity. 'She does!' Angel rushed to protest earnestly. 'I know what it feels like to think you're nothing but a nuisance.' Feeling awkward at the admission, she dodged his glance and added, 'I've never let Jas think for one second she isn't wanted and loved.'

'I'm sure you're a great mother, but that isn't the issue.'

He thinks I'm a great mother? 'What is the issue, Alex?' It was pretty obvious that the superficial similarities had dredged up some old issues for him. 'This isn't about your relationship with your father. You can't allow the things that happened in the past to colour the present.'

He emitted a laugh of disbelief. 'So it's purely accidental that your mothering style is the complete opposite of your own mother's? That's not a criticism, it's a fact. It's what people do. We try to avoid our parents' mistakes. Some of us fail....'

He gave a snort of self-disgust. 'Talk about history repeating itself.'

'That's not true! The situations are totally different,' she protested.

'In as much as Lizzie's mother chose not to tell my father she was pregnant because she knew he was married. You didn't even know my name. My dad had always been my hero. He made a real effort with me, maybe to compensate for the fact he'd been estranged from his own father. We did everything together, then afterwards... It was never the same between us. I didn't hold back. I let him know I despised him. I never lost an opportunity to twist the knife. Pretty ironic considering that I ended up emulating him.'

'But you didn't!' she exclaimed. 'You're not—!'

His blue eyes lifted and Angel could see that they blazed with self-contempt in the half-light. 'Married...? My wife had been dead weeks! Tell me how that makes me any better?'

The pain in his voice made her wince. 'People do things when they're grieving that they wouldn't do normally.'

A sound of astonishment escaped his lips as he moved towards her out of the shadows. 'You're trying to excuse what I did...?' He swallowed, the muscles in his brown throat visibly working as he finished on a note of raw incredulity, '*You* of all people!'

'You're not being fair on yourself, Alex. You loved your wife, you were hurting, grieving... You had been for a long time....'

'I knew it was going to happen.'

'And is that meant to make it easier? For goodness' sake, Alex, cut yourself some slack.' She registered his startled expression but didn't let it faze her or allow him the space to protest. Some things needed saying, especially when they were so obvious, and he was too close to it. 'You were there when your wife needed you, weren't you?'

'I think so.... Yes, I was, but I couldn't...'

'I know that's hard, but you tried and you did your best. And when she was gone you did something out of character, not because you loved her any less, but because you wanted to stop...thinking.' She shook her head sadly. 'I don't know what your wife was like, but I'm willing to bet she would have understood what you did and not considered it any sort of betrayal. I wouldn't, if it had been me.'

She was displaying a generosity of spirit that made him feel humble. 'I think you are a better person than me.'

'I wish I was. You lost yourself in one night of sex and I...I...' She choked with a bitter laugh. 'I was kind of in love with the idea of being in love. Relax,' she added, seeing his expression. 'I have grown up.'

'Being a single parent will do that to a person.' She might have relieved some of his guilt over that night but not over the repercussions. 'I want my child to know she is wanted, Angel.' He doubted very much he could be as good a father as Angel was a mother, but he would try.

'So why didn't you just say so instead of... It's obvious your sister had a tough time, but Jasmine knows she is wanted, Alex.'

'She doesn't know she is wanted by me.'

The words made her heart give a heavy thud of empathy. In the fast-falling dark she struggled to read his expression. Now his figure was little more than a dark outline, backlit by the moonlight reflected off the silvered ocean surface.

'You wanted me to listen.... Angel, I'm listening. I want to help, I want to be involved. Is that selfish? I don't know….' He took a deep breath, a soft sibilant hiss escaping through his teeth before he said quietly, 'No threats.'

'I wasn't threatened.' Not true—she had been. But not nearly as much as she would have been had she not had the security and the confidence of a brother with all the ruthlessness and resources to face Alex on equal terms. To fight on her behalf, should she ask him.

'I need to be part of her life…whatever it takes.'

Angel's restless covetous glance was drawn and then lingered on the sculpted contours of his wide, sensual mouth.

There was a big difference, she reminded herself, between wanting and needing. She needed to rediscover that mouth about as much as she needed a boil on her nose, but, God, she wanted it so much it hurt.

Angling her chin defiantly, she cleared her throat.

'I suppose you think all you have to do is kiss me and I'll agree to pretty much anything?' she challenged. 'Your problem is you think you're irresistible!' she tacked on, realising as she spoke that she was halfway to believing he was!

Maybe more than half, she thought. She recalibrated as she lost the ability to move, actually to breathe, as he surged towards her, taking the shallow steps of the bungalow veranda two at a time. He was at her side before she had an inkling of his intentions and then it was too late to stop him…. Did she actually want to?

He framed her face between his big hands. His stare had a soul-piercing intensity and she couldn't look away, afraid that a blink might break this spell.

'Kiss…?' The flash of his white grin was predatory as he bent his head and kissed her slowly, extending the erotic pleasure, taking his time as he slid his tongue deep between her parted lips, tasting her. There were no words to describe the sweet, hot ache between her thighs.

Angel was left gasping, open mouthed, for air when his head finally lifted. She felt his hands at her waist supporting her; her knees sagged; her legs felt as though they belonged to someone else.

'I'm planning to do more than kiss you, Angel,' he rasped, the promise making her tremble in anticipation. Still holding her eyes, he ran his tongue across the plump, trembling outline of her lower lip before tugging it gently with his teeth and asking, 'You have a problem with that?'

*His problem is he thinks he's God's gift!*
*My problem is he's right.*

In her head Angel saw herself pushing him away, defusing the situation with a few well-chosen words interspersed with the odd acid barb.

Outside her head, she was melting into him, pushing her aching breasts up hard against his chest, absorbing his heartbeat, his heat and the sheer maleness of him. She drew his head down so she could take the initiative and move her lips slowly across his, sampling the texture, breathing in his scent as, with eyes half-closed, she whispered into his mouth, 'No problem.'

His eyes flared and the primal incandescence made the breath in her lungs catch and burn. She stood trembling and passive, her heart thudding like a drum as he pushed his fingers deep into her lush hair so that they cradled her skull, dragging her head back to expose the long line of her throat.

Her eyelids squeezed tightly shut as he pressed his mouth to the pulse at the base of her throat. Her deep sigh became a long moan, the sound slipping past her clenched teeth as his tongue and lips progressed up her neck until he reached her mouth again. By this time her skin was slicked with a layer of moisture and she was panting short, shallow gasps as if she had just run a marathon.

Alex was breathing hard too as he brought his face in close. His nose grazing hers, she wrapped her arms around his neck, conscious of the rasp of each laboured inhalation. He was close enough for her to see the faint pinpoint marks left by sutures running either side of the thin white scar that was almost hidden by his hairline. His forehead was creased in a frown of intense concentration as he stared into her upturned features; the skin of his own face was drawn tight, pushing against the perfect bones, emphasising each individual plane and angle. He was breathtakingly beautiful, but it was the raw, rampant hunger stamped on his face that sent a fresh, explosive surge of sheer need coursing through Angel's body.

Struggling to articulate what she was feeling, simultaneously frightened and helplessly excited by the desire roaring like an out-of-control forest fire, in a voice that was hers, yet not hers, she whispered, 'I need this. I need you.'

Not her voice, but it was definitely his mouth that came crashing down on hers. Her body arched as she kissed him back, responding to the pressure with a wild frenzy of need that drew a deep, throaty moan from Alex.

'Hell, I don't have... We need to be careful.'

'No, it's fine. I'm on the pill.'

'Thank God!'

Still kissing frantically, they stumbled backwards. Angel was dimly aware of the sound of the door closing behind them a split second before she lost her footing and stumbled. Before she fell she was in his arms, swept quite literally off her feet, and being carried, a novel experience for a woman who was five-ten in her bare feet! A woman who had never before wanted to feel weak or helpless and out of control... That so wasn't her.

In the bedroom he rested one knee on the bed before he sat her down in the middle of the soft downy quilt. She rested there looking dazed and so beautiful that the box he had locked his feelings away in cracked wide open.

'You're beautiful,' he said, looking into the luminous, passion-glazed eyes lifted to his. He touched the side of her soft cheek with his thumb and felt her shiver. Her eyes drifted closed as she turned her head and, catching his wrist, pressed her lips to his palm.

The speed with which she had gone from hating him to feeling his pain and then wanting him more than oxygen was disorientating. Actually it was scary. 'This is me, not the airbrushed version.'

The warning drew an amused grunt. Alex abandoned the pretence he was in control as a wave of emotion moved through him. Instead he decided to enjoy it…and her.

'I have seen you naked before.'

Her eyes opened as he rose to his feet. She grabbed the front of his shirt and, falling backwards, pulled him with her.

She felt rather than heard his throaty chuckle as he raised himself on one arm and warned in a voice thickened by passion, 'I'll crush you.'

Still holding his shirt, she tugged—hard—smiling as pressure caused buttons to fly in all directions across the room. Hands flat on the delicious, warm golden skin of his chest, she leaned up to kiss him, tugging at the flesh of his lip with her teeth as she whispered, 'I'm kind of hoping you will.' The torrent of need he had awoken in her was elemental, out of control... *She* was out of control. The raw passion left no room in her head for any thought. She was driven, focused on one thing: to lose herself in him, to be totally consumed by his raw power.

Kneeling over her now, he didn't take his eyes off her face as he fought his way out of his shirt before flinging it across the room.

Her skin was so sensitised that even a light shiver made her conscious of every point of contact between her and her clothes. They felt heavy; she felt too hot.... She tugged at the neckline of her dress and tried to smooth the fabric bunched around her middle, barely able to breathe now as her eyes drifted hungrily over his naked torso and her quivering stomach muscles cramped. The heat crackling under her skin burned as she absorbed the details. He was utterly perfect: lean, hard, gold-toned skin gleamed with a slick of sweat; his broad chest had power and strength and was marked by whorls of dark hair and sharply defined with slabs of muscle; his belly was washboard flat and bisected by a directional arrow of dark hair. Her chest lifted in a deep, voluptuous sigh of appreciation.

The shirt long gone, moving quickly and urgently, Alex reached for the buckle on the narrow belt that was threaded through the waistband of the linen trousers he was wearing. But Angel was there before him, driven by an all-consuming need to feel him, see him, her fingers shaking but surprisingly nimble as they unclipped the belt.

Before she could follow through with the action, he took her hands and lifted them high above her head. He kissed her with slow, erotic thoroughness before he took hold of the thin top she wore and, taking the hem, lifted it over her head.

She was wearing a tiny pair of panties and a bra that was little more than a couple of triangles of lace in a matching pink.

Alex gave a low appreciative growl in his throat and reached for the catch on her bra.

The underwear was gone before her head hit the pillow and he was bending over her, stroking her, his hands moving down her sides and over her ribcage and up to cup the quivering flesh of her breasts. Her body arched up to meet him, her arms wrapping themselves around his neck, as she struggled to anchor her aching core to him, all the while pressing increasingly ardent kisses to the strong brown column of his neck.

Angel squeezed her eyes closed and sank her fingers into the deep lush pelt of his hair, extracting and relishing every individual sensation, but somehow it wasn't enough.

She wanted more; she needed more.

Maybe if she said it?

'I know.' His breath was moist and hot on her cheek, on her neck then her breast, and the air left her lungs in one open-mouthed gasp. His hands were moving up over her ribcage as his tongue traced the outline of her areola, before drawing the engorged peaks into his mouth first one, then the other.

In a fever of need she only distantly registered him sliding her panties down over her hips, gasping but not resisting as he parted her legs. She moaned low in her throat, pushing against his hand as he slid his fingers between her legs, parting the swollen and incredibly sensitive folds, making her pant and gasp as he rhythmically stroked the swollen flesh. Her gasps turned to deep feral moans as he touched the tight nub at her core and her body lifted off the bed.

'You like that?'

She nodded. It made her dizzy to look into his burning eyes but she knew that the trust required to let him touch her went way beyond the merely physical. She had a connection with this man who was the father of her child, and that made it neither shocking nor shameful.

She lifted her head and kissed him back hungrily, no longer even attempting to retain control. She didn't want control; she wanted wild and elemental. She wanted Alex, wanted to be devoured, absorbed, to become one with him.

'I want you too!'

Had she spoken out loud?

'Hell, I haven't been able to think straight,' he groaned, 'since I saw that photo of you.' Holding her eyes with his as they lay side by side, he took her hand and curled her fingers around his hard, smooth shaft. 'That's how much I want you, Angel,' he slurred thickly.

He felt so good, and his half-closed eyes

gleamed feverishly bright as she touched him. His expression turned raw and predatory and aroused her more than she had imagined possible.

Her lips parted as he lowered his mouth to hers, the deep, probing kiss draining her, sending her deeper and deeper into a vortex of sensation. As he moved over her she reached down and guided him into her, holding his gaze until that last moment when he slid thick and hard inside her.

Her eyes squeezed closed as every cell of her being focused on the feeling. She heard herself gasp.

'Oh, please!' As they began to move together his hands anchored her hips to the bed and she wrapped her long thighs tightly around him. Breathless, Angel moved with him, her sweat-slicked skin gliding and sliding against his. Their gasps and cries merged into one as their bodies came together, until she gave herself up to the firestorm of wild sensation that rocked her body.

As she began to float back down to earth Angel felt light. The secret burdens she had carried all her life were gone. She had slain her demons, she wasn't her mother—she loved him.

She lay in the dark, appreciating what had happened to her, not being afraid of it any more than she was afraid of her own heartbeat. He was as much a part of her as that. That he didn't feel the same way, that he couldn't, made her sad, but it also made her determined to extract every last atom of pleasure from the moment.

There were more moments during the night, less urgent, less bruisingly raw perhaps, but each one more shatteringly sensual than the last.

Angel woke feeling cold. The sheet was crumpled on the floor and Alex was lying on the other side of the bed. He woke as she shuffled across the bed and shivered as she pushed closer to the warmth of his body. Streaks of light had appeared along the wide horizon where the sea met the sky. It would soon be morning and what then…?

She shivered again and felt her chest tighten with an emotion she identified as loneliness. How crazy. She wasn't alone—she had Jas. A sigh hissed from her lips.

'Are you cold?'

'I'm fine,' she said, her voice muffled against his shoulders. He threw his arm across her and it lay big and heavy and reassuring across her shoulders. She liked the feel of his hair-rough-ened thigh against her smooth leg.

*Don't get to like it too much, Angel,* the voice in her head advised. Turning a deaf ear to that voice, she focused on the fingers that were moving in slow, lazy, circular movements across her belly.

Then the hand stilled and she sensed the tension in his body. 'What is that?'

She shivered, this time with pleasure as the heel of his hand rested on the sensitive mound of her pubic bone, though he ran his thumb along the thin white line not quite obscured by the soft fuzz of curls at the apex of her long legs.

'Complications during labour. I had an emergency C-section.'

He felt as if a hand had reached into his chest. So much had happened to her that he was responsible for and he'd been totally oblivious.

'You could have died?' Guilt rose like bile in his throat. What had he been doing at the time? Driving a fast car? Signing off on a deal and congratulating himself? Enjoying technically perfect sex with a beautiful woman…?

There had been nothing technical about last night. Raw, explosive, elemental—yes; as addictive as a narcotic—definitely! He knew now why he had gone to such lengths to bring her back into his life. He'd been trying to recapture this feeling, this emotional connection that only a single one-night stand had given him.

'If I'd been living in a Third World country possibly, but I wasn't. It was all routine.' And scary as hell.

He didn't believe a word of it. He had taken her innocence and got her pregnant. *A prince among men, that's you,* Alex told himself.

'You were alone?'

She shook her head.

'Your mother was with you?'

The suggestion drew a chortle of laughter from Angel.

'I thought maybe having a baby would have brought you together.'

Her hands curled over his. Drawing his fingers to her lips, she kissed them, then his mouth. Some breathless moment later she admitted with a laugh, 'Being old enough to be a grandmother is a crime my mother has still not forgiven me for. I'm not even sure what country she was in when I gave birth. She bores easily.'

He said a word that sounded vicious.

'Will you teach me to swear in Russian? That sounds really satisfying.'

'If you teach me to make love in Italian, *cara*.'

'It works for me.'

'Tell me you weren't alone when you gave birth.'

'I wasn't,' she said, hearing the guilt in his request. 'My friend, Clara.' Who despite her very good intentions had spent the first few hours of Angel's forty-eight-hour labour flirting with a young doctor, and when things had started happening had fainted away gracefully. While the labour had gone disastrously wrong, Clara was being diagnosed with concussion and even got admitted overnight. Angel had been her maid of honour when her friend had married the handsome young obstetrician six months later.

'And my brother flew back from Dubai as soon as he got the news I was in labour. Jas arrived a month early, so he was there to hold her before I came around.' According to the midwives he had worn a trench in the floor walking up and down, waiting for her to recover from the anaesthetic.

*That should have been me.* The thought surfaced, the strength of it taking him by surprise. He should have held his baby, and now he never would. His loss, not hers. It was obvious that Angel put her child above all else.

She omitted a few details from her potted history, such as that she'd come around in a high-dependency unit, or that her first recollection when she had surfaced from the anaesthetic had been hearing her forceful sibling who had no doubt bullied the information out of the doctor asking him if he was sure she would never be able to have children in the future.

'Is there no hope? IVF...?'

'Not impossible but extremely unlikely,' had been the medic's response. 'Would you like me to tell the father...? Or will you...?'

'If I ever find the scum who did this to her I'll do better than that! I'll make sure he doesn't do this to any other woman! Is she awake yet?'

Angel, who had closed her eyes and pretended to be unconscious, had almost immediately drifted back into a drug-induced slumber.

But when she'd woken she had remembered the conversation she had overheard, which had helped when Cesare had broken the news to her later; she had been able to make it easier for him by responding calmly as she'd told him honestly that she was fine. When she'd been discharged a few days later everyone had considered her to be coping remarkably well, though Angel had been unable to dispel the feeling that they were waiting for her to fall apart.

When they'd realised she wasn't going to—it had taken a while—it had been a relief that everyone had stopped walking on eggshells around her and she could get on with looking after her baby. She had happily left the anger to her brother, who had deduced with no help or confirmation from her that the father was married.

She had genuinely believed she was all right until that morning six months down the line when she had been folding away the clothes that Jasmine had outgrown, smoothing the fabric of a hand-knitted, exquisite, tiny newborn cardigan that it was hard to believe her robust bouncing daughter had ever fitted into. The reality had hit her with no warning.... Why was she storing the tiny garment so carefully in layers of tissue and lavender bags for the future? There would be no brother or sister to wear it.

No more babies.

The tears had begun to leak from her eyes, silently at first, then had come the muffled sobs and finally the awful wrenching wails. A lot later she had dried her eyes and the next day had delivered all the baby clothes to the local charity shop, reminding herself sternly that she had a precious child and many people were not that lucky.

She had not thought of it since, but now she realised that she had needed to cry, needed to mourn a future that was lost, she thought sadly. But she had done her mourning and moved on; now she was getting on with her life.

Had Alex? Was he still mourning the future with his wife that had been denied him?

'Was your wife ill a long time?'

She felt him stiffen a moment before he rolled away from her. 'Yes.'

'I know mourning is a very personal process.' She reached out to stroke his back before taking a deep breath and beginning tentatively, 'My friend had grief counselling when her—'

'I don't need a grief counselor. I have you. You were right—I have been eaten with guilt because I buried my grief in anonymous sex. I'm not proud of it but you helped me see...I have moved on, Angel. The question is,' he said quietly, 'have you?'

In the space of a heartbeat Angel experienced the disorientating sensation of a total role reversal. One second she was feeling supportive and understanding, the next she was the one being asked to face her demons, and it was too soon.

## CHAPTER EIGHT

ANGEL HAD LAIN with her eyes closed, pretending to be asleep, as she heard him getting dressed. But when she heard Alex moving around in the other room she got up. She didn't want him to leave without doing something to close the distance that had opened up between them.

Belting her robe, she walked quietly into the adjoining room. Alex, who hadn't heard her, was holding the photo of Jasmine in the silver frame. It was the expression she saw etched on his face in the brief moment before he realised she was there that swung it—the longing mixed with pain that vanished the moment he knew he was not alone.

Swallowing the lump of emotion in her throat and ignoring the small voice in her head that told her she'd live to regret opening this door, she responded to his cautious good morning with, 'You can see Jas.'

He went rigid for a moment, his face a total blank, then he smiled and tipped his head. 'Good.'

'If you agree that when and how to tell her who you are is my call.'

Slowly he nodded. 'That seems fair.'

Angel expelled a deep sigh and hoped like hell once more that this was going to work out.... She had to make it work. 'Right, I'll make arrangements. Another thing I think that—no!' She backed away shaking her head, one arm extended as if to fend him off as he approached, the gleam in his eyes sending her nervous system into meltdown. 'Don't!'

His fingers that had moved to loosen the knot on her robe stopped; he was frustrated but not alarmed. He bent his head towards her. 'What's wrong?'

Wrong, yes, she thought, that was the right word. He'd been the wrong man at the wrong time for all the wrong reasons.

'I can't.'

The furrow on his brow smoothed. 'You have an early call? That's a pity,' he murmured, thinking it was a disaster! Unable to stop himself, he dropped his eyes to the thrusting profile of her nipples. He had never wanted a woman as much as he did Angel. It was a struggle to present a casual attitude about this delay when every cell in his body was pumped and primed to peel back the layer of silk and explore the even silkier delights beneath.

'I don't have an early call. I mean… What I mean…' She stopped, squeezed her eyes closed and groaned. 'Don't look at me like that,' she pleaded.

'Like what?'

His display of innocence drew a growl of frustration from Angel. 'Like you're…'

'Thinking about making love to you…?'

When wasn't he?

His eyes narrowed as he struggled to contain a flicker of shock. Sex no longer came with a big guilt trip. It had become a normal part of his life again, but it was not something that occupied his thoughts exclusively. Or it hadn't been until Angel had come back into his life.

This frank translation made her flush and press a hand to her heaving chest.

'I can't focus!' she choked. 'I'm trying to tell you we can't…ever do…' she jerked her head in the direction of the open bedroom door where the tumbled bedclothes were visible '...that.'

'That?'

She lifted her chin and responded to his taunt with an unintentionally loud reply. 'Sex. That's part of the deal. If you want to be part of Jas's life then we have to get our act together.' She expelled a breath. It was over with; she had said it. This was the point where the tension was meant to flow from her body. She had told herself she'd feel better once she got this over with, but she didn't.

'You just lost me.'

She struggled to preserve her calmness, aware in the face of this pretence of ignorance that with his steel-trap mind he got the point half an hour before most people. 'A child needs continuity... security.'

What she did not need was a constant stream of 'uncles' at the breakfast table; she did not need slammed doors, raised voices, dramas played out at volume at all hours of the day and night; she did not need spurned lovers who turned nasty or even the ones that turned pathetic.

'You expect me to argue with that?'

'I put Jas's needs ahead of my own,' she said quietly.

There might not be a definitive rule book that told you how to be a good mother—Angel had discovered everyone had to work it out for themselves, and there were times when she frankly got it wrong and worried about just how much mothering skills were down to genes—but at least she knew how not to be a bad mother, or at least an uninterested one.

Growing up, she would have settled for her mother remembering once in a while that she had children! Her beautiful and erratic parent had lived her life exactly as she had wanted and her children had been the ones who had done the adapting.

'And you need me.'

The smug insertion proved to Angel that they were still not on the same page. 'This isn't about your ego,' she flared, tightening the belt on her robe, thus unwittingly causing the neckline to gape.

Jaw clenched, Alex dragged his gaze off the heaving contours of her bosom and the effort made his tone abrupt.

'Then what is it...?' He stopped as the penny belatedly dropped. He could see where this was going.

'You mean you want to get married?'

The cynic in him was not surprised. It was not the first time a woman had looked at him as prospective husband material. He was normally alert to the subtle signs that signalled attempts to manoeuvre him into matrimony, but he hadn't seen this one coming. For some reason, neither could he summon up his well-rehearsed smile, the one that softened his harsh response.

And none of the women he had let down gently had been the mother of his child.

His eyes narrowed. That made a difference. And now that he thought of it, was it such a bad idea from a purely practical point of view? Of course he was old-fashioned enough to prefer to be the one making the proposal, but Angel's horrified exclamation suddenly cut into his stream of thought.

'M-marry? Of course not!'

The unmitigated horror in her voice was reflected on her face. It seemed he could always rely on Angel to deliver a kick to his ego.

'That would be ridiculous.' She gave a laugh, wincing when her effort to convince him she was neither crazy nor an idiot made her sound both. 'I'm not wife material, believe me.'

'What, parents getting married?' His jaw clenched as he resisted the childish impulse to inform her that there were more than a few women who would not consider the idea of being his bride a nightmare. 'Hell, yes, you're right, crazy…that would never catch on,' he drawled, swinging away from her, his feet silent on the floor as he stalked towards the window. He reminded her of a caged tiger on a short leash as he traversed the room.

'Please, this is not a joke,' she reproached to his retreating back.

He spun back, spearing the fingers of both hands deep into his hair as he rocked back on his heels. 'Sorry.'

Her eyes narrowed. 'Thanks for that sincerity.'

'I'm sincere—sincerely tired of this ridiculous discussion.' His sarcasm made Angel clench her teeth. 'Just tell me what is bothering—'

'My pretty little head?' she jumped in, glaring.

A spasm of irritation crossed his patrician features. 'You are not pretty.'

Angel was not particularly mad about her looks. Given the choice she would have chosen blonde and petite, but she had no body-image issues and she was well aware that she was considered by most people to be more than averagely attractive, so it made it all the more crazy that the comment hurt. 'So I'm ugly!' She could not believe this childish response was coming from her own mouth.

'No, you are beautiful,' he countered. Midglare his eyes broke contact with Angel's and slid to the photo. 'So is she. She looks so like you....'

The husky observation successfully refocused Angel's attention. 'She has a much sweeter temperament.'

'Maybe she takes after her father...?'

Alex Arlov, sweet? Any other time the two words in the same sentence would have had her in hysterics but Angel didn't crack a smile.

She made an effort to channel calm. 'I can't have an affair with you, Alex.'

Even if she could have stomached the idea of sex without an emotional commitment it wouldn't have worked. She simply lost all sense of perspective when it came to Alex. She could never maintain any sort of simple sexual relationship with the way he made her feel.

She had never understood women who would risk everything for a man. She didn't want to understand, but what she did know was that if such a man existed Alex Arlov was the living, breathing embodiment of it.

'Who's saying I want an affair?'

She flinched at the growled rebuttal and, lifting her chin, defiantly murmured, 'My mistake.' Presumably an affair was too formal a footing for what he had in mind. 'As a matter of interest, what did you have in mind?' She arched a delicate brow and suggested in a sardonic drawl, 'Friends with benefits?'

'We are not friends.'

'Thank you for reminding me.'

A look of regret slid across his lean face. 'I didn't mean it that way.... I just...' He dragged a hand through his dark, tousled hair. 'I just... You're driving me crazy.'

There's a lot of it around, Angel thought grimly. 'Don't worry, I appreciate bluntness,' she said instead. Hopefully he could take it as well as dish it out. 'I can't have sex with you at all. We need to keep our relationship uncomplicated for Jasmine.'

He struggled to follow her logic and realised there was none. 'How is us sleeping together bad for Jasmine?'

'I want my daughter to learn about relationships based on mutual respect and—'

'Our daughter.'

The correction made her grate her teeth. 'For five years she's been my daughter, Alex.'

'And you resent the fact it has to change,' he flung.

The suggestion that this was a *fait accompli* annoyed her. He was failing to recognise that she was the one making an effort.

'I'm an example to my daughter. I don't want her to think casual sex is all she can have. I watched my mother sleep her way around the fashionable spots of Europe. I had her boyfriends drift in and out of my life and I don't want that sort of instability for Jasmine.'

'So you *are* holding out for marriage.' He seized on this evidence triumphantly.

'I'm holding out for a relationship based on

more than lust,' she countered. 'One that is… safe.'

His heavy-lidded gaze slid over her sleek, sensuous curves and the fist of desire in his belly tightened. 'Safe!' he spat in disgust. 'And what is so terrible about lust? Lust is not a bad place to start.…' he commented in a deep throaty drawl that made the surface of her skin tingle.

The deep, drowning blue of his eyes made her dizzy and it was an effort to break the contact. 'Only if both participants want the same thing.'

'I thought I gave you what you wanted.'

His inability to see what she was saying drew a frustrated grunt from Angel.

'My mother changed her lovers the way some women change their shoes. I know what it feels like to grow fond of someone and have them vanish or to hear arguments when you're trying to go to sleep, to have a sleazy boyfriend of your mother's make a pass at you.' She saw the outrage flare in his eyes and added quickly, 'Only once and my brother walked in.'

'So how is the fact your mother was a lousy parent relevant?'

'I know what bad parenting is.'

'And good parenting involves being some sort of born-again virgin? I'm curious—are you planning on not having any sex or is it just sex with me that will emotionally scar our daughter?'

'You're deliberately twisting things.'

'So untwist things and tell me you're not saying I can either be part of my daughter's life or sleep with you?'

'It is not an either-or situation, Alex.'

He exhaled a frustrated hiss through his teeth. 'What is it, then?' Without waiting for her to respond, he shook his head and, drawing a sharp line in the air with his hand, said, 'You know, I really don't want to hear, because none of it is true. You know what I think? I think this isn't about Jasmine, it's about you. You're using her as an excuse because underneath that facade you're scared. What of? Becoming your mother?'

'Of course not,' she answered too quickly.

'From what you've told me you are the exact opposite of your mother.'

'This isn't about my mother. It's about us.... You.'

'You're scared of me?' A look of shock chased across his lean face. 'It never occurred to me you were… Why would you be?' His eyes narrowed as her eyes slid from his, shifting to a point over his shoulder. It was a telling gesture.

'Of course not.' It was true, she wasn't afraid of Alex, but she was afraid of the way he made her feel. The emotional impact of meeting him again had felt like having a tourniquet removed from a deadened limb and the abrupt resumption of circulation and feeling had been agonising. But as hard as she'd tried she couldn't reapply the tourniquet to her emotions.

She loved him and he was going to break her heart. It was as inevitable as night following day. But it wasn't the broken heart precisely that she was avoiding—it was Jasmine witnessing it breaking, seeing the slow disintegration of the relationship and thinking, as Angel had, that that was all there was to look forward to in life.

'We all have issues in our childhood….'

The insensitive attempt at amateur psychology brought her resentful gaze back to his face. A second was all it took for him to capture and hold her.

'What made you so scared of enjoying a normal healthy sex life?'

'I'm not afraid,' she replied, hiding her discomfiture behind a cool mask.

'Did your father cheat on your mother?' he speculated.

'My dad adored my mother even after she walked out on their marriage and took us with her, then did her level best to forget we existed.' In a small corner of her head a voice was saying, 'Too much information, Angel!' but she couldn't stem the flow of revelations. 'And in answer to your question, I'm not scared, I'm determined—determined that my daughter will always be my first priority.'

She gave a weary sigh. 'It's simply the way I want it to be. Don't you see?' she appealed to him. 'This,' she said, moving her hand in an illustrative sweep from her chest to him and back again, 'is exactly the situation I want to avoid.'

'This is a situation that you have engineered,' he countered grimly. 'You've created a self-fulfilling prophesy. Do you even know how unrealistic you're being? Do you really think you're going to find some guy you'll never fight with? You'd be bored within a week,' he predicted.

'I'm not looking for a guy. This is just the way it's going to be, take it or leave it.'

It was the torment in her green eyes that made him hold his tongue—that and the realisation that she genuinely believed all the rubbish she was spouting. Her logic was totally crazy but he recognised this might not be the time to point it out. This was the time for a tactical retreat...but he would be back.

Alex closed the door behind him as he left, which should have made her happy. It was what she wanted, but as she picked up the phone to arrange Jasmine's trip over to meet her father happiness was not the emotion that was uppermost in her mind. She might never have sex again, and that was reason enough to feel depressed.

She had had the most gorgeous man in the universe ask her to be with him, and she had sent him away! More significantly, he had gone without even putting up much of a fight.... Probably, she thought gloomily, he'd been secretly relieved.

But she'd done the right thing, almost definitely she'd done the right thing. They'd made a great child, but living together… No, she had made the right decision…totally!

Wasn't the right thing meant to make you feel good?

She didn't feel good; she felt like someone who had just slammed the doors of paradise shut and stayed on the wrong side, which was mad because paradise was a cool, calm place of serenity. Serene and Alex… No, she had made the right decision, hadn't she…?

She lifted her chin and took a deep breath. *For God's sake, Angel, you've made your bed and now you have to lie in it…alone.*

Things happened faster than Angel had anticipated. The young woman who was standing in for her nanny was available to accompany Jasmine on the next flight, and she seemed eager to. So it was less than twenty-four hours later that she was thanking her for accompanying Jasmine on the journey and saying goodbye, leaving her to wait for her return flight.

Jasmine, strapped into the seat beside her, was so excited she chatted constantly all the way from the airport, unable to keep still in the seat.

When they reached the bungalow she was visibly flagging.

'You like your bedroom?' Angel asked as the little girl did her umpteenth circuit of the room.

'Love it loads,' she said, taking a seat on the bed, watching while Angel unpacked her small suitcase. Jasmine began to swing her legs metronome style, her heels hitting the wooden frame with a regular dull thud.

'These shorts are too tight,' she remarked as Angel took out a blue denim pair with cute ducks on the patch pockets. 'But we didn't have any time to buy some more.'

'Don't worry, we'll buy you some new ones. There you go—all done,' Angel said as she put the last T-shirt in the drawer and closed it. 'How about a nap?'

The little girl looked offended. 'I'm not a baby, and I want to go in the water. You promised.'

Angel sighed. Like an elephant, her daughter never forgot. 'Everyone has naps in the afternoon in warm countries.'

'Even grown-ups?'

Angel nodded. 'Absolutely.'

'So you're going to take a nap too…with me?'

The logic was inescapable, and Angel, knowing a rash promise once made was hard to escape, dodged the issue.

'Why don't you change into your swimsuit and we'll have a swim first?' She floated the idea, knowing what the response would be. Watching her daughter leap up and down like a crazy thing on the bed made her realise how quiet her life was without Jas in it, how much emptier.

This was her. This was what she wanted, but did Alex, with his billionaire jet-setting lifestyle, have a clue what he was asking for?

Having left Jas to change into her swimsuit, Angel changed into her own one-piece—a black halter that she double tied at the neck. The last time she had been wearing it in a public pool, Jas had thought it funny to unfasten the bow and Angel had found herself in a very embarrassing topless situation.

He was nervous.

Alex gave a self-derisive smile. He was nervous of meeting a five-year-old child! Maybe nervous was not the best word to describe the combination of excitement, anticipation and trepidation in his gut. Carrying the gift—it had been a novel, actually a unique, experience for Alex to pick out a gift personally and not delegate the task to his excellent PA—he walked along the beach towards Angel's bungalow. He was a few hundred yards away when he heard the sound of laughter.

He did not consciously follow the sound but he ended up on the shore, oblivious to the waves lapping over his leather shoes, watching the two playing a game that involved much splashing and lots of noise. The first glimpse of his daughter was as Angel lifted her high out of the water, a wriggling laughing figure whose high-pitched chuckle he could hear above Angel's husky contralto tone.

There were few perfect moments in life, the really golden ones that stayed with you until the end. Alex had read somewhere that witnessing the birth of your child was considered by many to be one of them. He had not been there for the birth of his child so in some ways this was it: perfect. She was perfect.

'Who is that man, Mummy?'

Angel, who had just surfaced from the water and was kneeling, turned her head and saw him.

Her stomach flipped. She had never associated the word lonely with Alex Arlov but standing there he looked… She swallowed the boulder lodged in her aching throat and slowly got to her feet.

'That's my friend.' She extended her hand to Jasmine. 'Shall we go say hello?'

Alex remembered a friend who had described how unreal it had felt to take his newborn home from hospital for the first time. He had spoken of the shock of overnight becoming, not a couple, but a family.

Times that by a million, Alex thought, and you might get somewhere near the complex swirl of emotions he was feeling.

He wasn't seeing a new baby. His daughter was not a blank slate; she was a fully formed little person with a store of experiences that he knew nothing about, a personality. Was she scared of the dark? He resented that he didn't know, but he was going to find out, and the only way to do that was to be a family.

Alex believed that only fools rushed headlong into important decisions, and allowing emotions to become involved was just so obviously a massive mistake that it did not even warrant debate. It turned out there were exceptions to this rule and standing on the beach he discovered one. He made the most important decision in his life without a second's debate or hesitation.

He was going to marry Angel and they were going to be a family. It would happen.

# CHAPTER NINE

J ASMINE ACCEPTED THE explanation without question. 'Does he want to play with us?'

Angel shook her head. 'I don't think so, sweetheart, and I think maybe we've had enough now too.' She took her daughter's hand and they waded out of the shallows and onto the beach where Alex, his dark hair fluttering slightly in the breeze, was standing looking gorgeous. This was obviously a given, but he was also incongruous in this setting in a tailored pale grey suit. The top button of his white silk shirt open and his tie hanging loose around his neck were the only minor concessions to the sun beating down.

His appearance was not lost on Jasmine.

'Your shoes are wet. It's really stupid to wear shoes on the beach.' She wriggled her own bare toes in the wet sand and directed her critical gaze to the rest of him. She didn't seem impressed by what she was seeing. 'Or a suit. It's not p-pract...?'

She looked to her mother, who automatically supplied the word, 'Practical,' before adding, 'Don't be rude, Jas.'

Alex stepped back out of the shallow water, barely giving his handmade Italian-leather shoes a glance. His daughter had a Scottish accent; the highland lilt was unmistakable. It brought home forcibly the extent of his ignorance. He didn't even know where she had lived her five years. He had assumed London, but clearly he couldn't have been more wrong.

'She's right. My outfit is not beach appropriate.' His outfit was appropriate for the discussion of oil leases. If the change of venue had been considered unusual by the oil executives who had expected to be in London, they had not said so when he had met the fleet of helicopters personally. 'But I've been working, and you, I see, have been swimming.'

'I can't swim yet. Mum has tried to teach me but I'm not a natural.'

Her sigh and serious expression drew a smile from Alex. While he did not know a lot about five-year-olds it seemed to him as a not-totally-objective observer that his daughter was pretty advanced for her age, and she not only looked startlingly like her mother but she was also not afraid of speaking her mind.

'Perhaps I could teach you?'

He turned his head towards Angel to gauge her reaction to his suggestion. She was bending forward to pick up a towel from the sand, a wet swathe of her hair concealing her face.

'Mummy?'

Angel dropped the towel around her shoulders. 'That's very kind.' The little girl skipped ahead.

'So do you mind?'

'That's not the point. You made it impossible for me to say no, and I don't appreciate that. Don't manipulate me, Alex.'

'It wasn't intentional. She didn't look to be afraid of the water.'

Angel laughed. 'Jas isn't afraid of anything. That's the problem—she has very little sense of danger. I don't want to make her scared but it's a hard balance…. She's not afraid of water. It's the cold—she hates it. I first tried to teach her at home when she was a toddler—we have the white sand and the clear seas, but the water is not warm at any time of the year and she is a warm-blooded little creature. She loves the sun.'

'So I see. The accent came as a surprise—charming, but a surprise.'

'I don't even notice she has an accent. We have an apartment in the castle….' She saw Alex's expression and added a quick explanatory footnote, 'My brother inherited the estate when our dad died—beautiful, remote and a lot of rain. Isn't it every little girl's dream to live in a castle?'

'Is it?'

'I was happy there when I was her age.'

'You have no accent.'

Her smile faded. 'No, I lost it and my roots, but Jasmine won't.'

'Roots are less about places and more about people.'

'There speaks someone who didn't grow up in a series of hotel rooms.'

'You said she had been ill? Was it serious?'

'It took a while to diagnose, a thing with her hip. It required a lot of bed rest and that was tough. They thought she might be left with a limp but she's fine. Are you all right, Alex?'

He tore his eyes off the playing child and nodded. 'Fine.' As fine as any man could be when he knew the woman he loved had faced all those things alone.

'Are you sure?'

He nodded. 'I should have been there.'

The burning intensity of his gaze made her look away. 'You're here now.'

'Yes, I am.'

They caught up with Jasmine, who, to Angel's maternal eyes, was showing visible signs of flagging. 'Want a carry, sweetheart?'

'No, I'm okay. What's that?' She stared curiously at the parcel in Alex's hand.

He withdrew the book from behind his back. 'A book. I thought you might like it. It's about a princess who marries a handsome prince after he saves her from a dragon.' A far simpler time when all a man had to do to prove himself was slay the odd dragon. Life was much more complicated these days.

'I already have a book about a princess. She rescues the prince and she hates pink.'

A lot more complicated—he couldn't even impress a five-year-old. 'It seems,' Alex said in a soft rueful aside to Angel as she took the book from him, 'that I am not politically correct enough.'

They had reached the steps to the bungalow and Angel opened the book. 'Look, Jas, this book has such lovely pictures, really beautiful.' How crazy that she wanted to save his feelings. He was trying so hard that it made her heart ache to watch him.

'Are there any cats in it?'

'I'm not sure,' Alex admitted.

'I like cats. Thank you very much.'

He inclined his head. 'You are most welcome, Jasmine.'

She allowed herself to be led up the steps to the veranda, where she jumped directly onto a bench. 'I could look at the pictures now.'

'Nice try. We had a deal. A swim and then a nap.'

With a show of reluctance she got up.

'Say goodnight to Alex.'

'Goodnight, Mr Alex.'

'Goodnight, Jasmine.'

'There's a bottle of wine open in the fridge if you want some. I won't be long…if you want to wait.'

'I want…'

He stood up when Angel walked back into the living room a few minutes later and pulled out a chair for her, wincing as it scraped on the wooden floor. 'Sorry.'

'Don't worry. Nothing will wake her now.'

'She's quite a character. You have done a good job.'

Angel felt herself blush with pleasure at the compliment. 'I've had a lot of help.…'

'You have a nanny?'

Her chin lifted defensively. 'Luckily.'

He watched, one brow raised, as she ignored the wine he had poured and filled her coffee cup from a Thermos jug. 'It was not a criticism.'

'My brother is great and my normal nanny is sporting a leg plaster. Her really great stand-in flew over with Jas and then back.'

'So what does your brother do—?' He broke off, frowning. 'Is that a good idea?' She looked at him over the rim of her cup. 'You do know you're displaying all the classic signs of caffeine overload?'

'Am I?'

'You're jumpy as hell, you can't sit still…

Look,' he broke off to say as the cup she had put back down on the table rattled. 'You're trembling and I bet your heart is racing and you're dizzy? Am I right?'

Oh, he was right. 'And that's because I drink too much coffee?' A man with a mind like a steel trap, but it turned out he didn't know everything. She was beginning to think that where she was concerned he knew nothing!

'If you're not careful...'

She gave a sputtering laugh and drew his frowning disapproval.

'This isn't funny, Angel.'

'Oh, I know it's not, believe me,' she said, looking at his mouth hard enough to memorise it. She picked up a magazine from the table and wafted her face with it. 'But don't worry, I know my limitations with coffee.' It was her limitations with Alex that were her problem. Her internal red light just failed to activate with him.

'You've met him, I think.'

He watched as she topped up her coffee cup. 'Who?'

'My brother. I believe you played with cars together. Cesare...?'

A look of utter astonishment spread across his face. 'You are Cesare Urquart's sister?' Meeting someone with a public persona in the flesh could, Alex knew, be disappointing when that person fell far short of your mental image. But that hadn't been the case when he had met the ex-racing driver whose career he had followed. He had liked the man and the feeling seemed to have been reciprocated.

She nodded.

'Does he know about me?' Alex asked, imagining his own reaction if the situation was reversed and he discovered the identity of the man who had got his young and beautiful sister pregnant.

'Not yet.'

'I'm assuming there will be no place to run,' he observed sardonically.

She flicked him a glance, resenting the fact he could look amused when she was genuinely worried about what her brother would do. Wade in all guns blazing probably.

'That settles it,' Alex said. 'I'll have to marry you.'

She struggled to match his flippancy. 'You really know how to sell the idea. Of course I'll marry you. Name the day.'

'Tomorrow, unless you want a big wedding?'

The joke was beginning to grow tired. 'Very funny.'

'Why would you think I'm joking?'

She turned to him with an astonished stare. 'Because if you weren't that would make you insane.'

'It is insane to think a child is better brought up within the confines of a marriage?'

'We're not talking about Jasmine.'

'Yes, we are, Jasmine and us. You won't be my lover, so be my wife.'

Feeling the panic begin to build, she pressed a hand to her tight chest. 'There is no us.'

A spasm of impatience moved across his lean face. 'Don't be ridiculous. I'm the father of your child and I'm the only man you've ever slept with. That adds up to a big fat us.'

'It doesn't add up to marriage.'

'I'm not talking a paper marriage, if that is what is bothering you. Not a sterile, convenient—' He saw her flinch and stopped. 'What have I said?'

Pale as paper, she shook her head. 'Too much.'

He shrugged and forced himself to stifle his impatience. He had given her enough to think about, planted the idea, now it would grow.

He allowed himself one final parting shot.

'You don't want Jasmine to be an only child, do you?'

She was glad he couldn't see her face, or the tears that began to slide down her cheeks. She was grateful to him; she needed that. For a moment there she had started to let herself think that the crazy things he said were possible.

# CHAPTER TEN

THE MOMENT ALEX walked into the hotel foyer, a trail of assistants behind him, he realised that something was wrong—it did not take a genius to work this out.

The area was crowded, some people talking, others gawking, and in the middle of them was Angel, white faced, wild eyed and she was shouting.

'What is wrong with you people? I don't want to sit down. I don't want to fill in a form. I've told you I can't find my daughter. My little girl, she was there and now she isn't. I need help, not tea!'

The shrill words stopped Alex in his tracks. He felt a cold hand close around his heart, then a moment later he was surging forward and the crowd was parting.

'Angel.'

She spun around; her expression when she saw

him would stay with him for ever. 'Thank God, Alex, it's Jas, she's—'

He laid his hands on her shoulders and held her eyes with his. 'I heard. Just tell me what happened.'

Angel expelled a deep shuddering sigh and focused on his eyes, trying to block out the rest of the room and the white noise of panic in her head. 'We were walking back after lunch.' She gave another deep sigh and shook her head.

'Look at me, Angel.'

She responded to the firm voice, taking comfort from the calm in it. 'She'd spent the morning at the shoot with me watching. We had lunch, yes, I already said that, and…I really should get back outside.'

'In a moment.'

'I saw Nico, he asked me about… I don't remember. I only turned away for a moment, really only a moment, and when I turned around she was gone, vanished!'

'And when was this?'

'A couple of… I don't know, just now.' She clutched her head and struggled to think straight, fighting her way through the panic.

'Fine. Show me where you last saw her.'

The next few minutes were a blur for Angel, who retraced her steps and repeated the sequence of events for what seemed like the thousandth time, then sat and watched, feeling helpless and more scared than she had imagined possible, while Alex divided up the volunteers into teams and gave them areas to cover.

'She can't have gone far, and ten teams can cover a lot of ground. We will find her.'

She caught his arm. 'I want to go too.'

'No, I need you and Nico to stay here in case she makes her own way back, and everyone has Nico's number.' Nico held up his phone. 'He's the contact so you'll be the first to know.'

'You're afraid you'll find something bad—that's why you don't want me to go!' she accused shrilly.

Alex took her by the shoulders. 'You can't think that way, Angel, and you're not going to fall apart. You're strong. Look at me, Angel.' Her wild restive gaze settled on his face. 'We are going to find her.'

She swallowed and took a deep shuddering breath. 'I'm not strong, Alex.'

He gave the most tender smile she had ever seen and touched her face. 'You are as tough as old boots.'

Then he was gone.

Nico's phone rang exactly ten minutes later, the longest ten minutes of her life.

Still holding his daughter's hand, Alex dropped into a squatting position beside her and pointed towards Angel, who was belting across the sand with Nico and several staff trailing in her wake. 'There's your mummy!'

As Angel reached them he released Jasmine's hand and, rising to his feet, took a step back as Angel, panting, tears streaming down her face, dropped down on her knees and grabbed Jasmine, hugging so tightly the little girl protested and wriggled to escape.

'Sorry...sorry...' Angel pushed her back, one hand patting her own mouth to hold back the sobs that struggled to escape from her throat as her anxious green eyes scanned her daughter's face. 'You're all right?' She lifted her eyes to the tall figure who stood over them both. 'She's a-all right? Oh, God, my teeth won't stop chattering.'

To witness the emotion she was leaking from every pore was making his throat ache. 'She's fine,' Alex promised huskily. 'She's just had a little adventure, haven't you, Jasmine? And none the worse for it, excepting a few scratches.'

'I was very, very brave.' She looked to Alex for confirmation of this proud boast and he tipped his head gravely.

'Just like your mother.'

Angel, shaking with the force of her relief, impelled to touch Jasmine every other second just to prove she was real, was not feeling brave. She was still fighting the nightmarish images in her head. As her distress began to communicate itself to the little girl the proud smile vanished and her lip began to tremble. 'Mummy…?'

'Don't do that again…ever…promise me.!'

Jasmine's face crumbled. 'You weren't there!' she wailed.

The words pierced Angel's heart. 'Don't cry, darling….' Angel sniffed, hugging her daughter's rigid body. 'It's all right now.' She stroked her daughter's head and Jasmine's arms went round her neck. Carrying her, Angel rose awkwardly to her feet and over the top of Jasmine's head she smiled at Alex and mouthed 'thank you'.

Cool focus and the ability to empty his mind of everything but what he needed to do had got Alex through this, had kept his darkest imaginings at bay. All it took was the gratitude in her shining eyes and those self-imposed barriers crumbled. He tipped his head, his own smile giving not a hint of the rush of powerful emotions locked tight in his chest, the primal need to protect the two women in his life from all the dangers that lurked out there.

He moved to stand protectively beside them and kissed the top of the curly head pressed to Angel's shoulder and said quietly, 'Will you be all right?'

Angel felt her face drop. 'You're not coming with us?' Hearing the wobble in her voice, she pinned on a weak smile in an effort to retrieve the situation, and she struggled to display some of the self-reliance she prided herself on.

All in all it was a pathetic effort.

His fingers tightened on the bones of her shoulder; his hand felt heavy, reassuring. Angel closed her eyes, sucked in a deep breath, before throwing her head back to meet his eyes.

'I'll be fine,' she pronounced, thinking, *Don't get used to leaning on him, Angel. He won't always be there.*

'I won't be long. I just want to make sure that this section of beach is fenced off by the morning. We don't want this happening again.' He sketched a bleak but determined smile and beckoned his nephew over. 'Nico will see you back to the bungalow and wait until I get back.'

Nico nodded. 'Of course.'

Jasmine raised her head. 'I want my kitten back.'

Angel arched a questioning brow and angled a glance up at Alex. 'Your kitten, darling?'

'She saw a stray cat and it looks like she followed it through the hole in the fence, crawled through after it. The cat led her back to her litter of feral kittens and Jasmine decided she wanted to take one home.' He skimmed over the struggle he had had to convince her that this was not a good idea. His daughter had, it seemed, inherited her mother's stubborn disposition as well as an underdeveloped sense of danger.

Life for a man in a household with two such fe-
males was not to be envied, but it was what Alex
had discovered he wanted for himself, what he
would do anything to achieve.

'Hence the scratches.'

'Scratches?'

He took one small grubby hand, turned it over,
and Angel saw the scratches on the chubby wrist
and arm. They looked red and angry. 'Hold on...'
He pulled his mobile phone out and glanced at
the message on the screen. 'Mark Lomas.'

Recognising the name of a man whom she had
exchanged the odd good morning with during the
week, Angel felt a stab of resentment that Alex
should consider taking a message from a guest
a priority at such a moment.

He gave a nod of satisfaction as he slid the
phone back into his breast pocket. 'Mark should
be there by the time you get to the bungalow.'

'Why?'

He felt a stab of anxiety as he studied her face
more closely. Angel remained dramatically pale,
her skin the colour of wax, her eyes dark emerald bruises nestled among the pallor.

He wanted to urge her to sit down before she

fell down and give him Jasmine, but he knew it would be a futile exercise. Angel was holding on to her daughter as if she would never let go and would definitely resist any efforts he made to lighten her burden.

His jaw tightened—a burden she had been carrying alone for too long because of him.

'I thought you might have spoken the other night. He's in the next bungalow to you. A doctor…?'

'I might have.'

'He's coordinating the medical backup on the charity race,' he explained, referring to the charity Ironman event that was currently causing a buzz in the hotel.

'I sent a text when I found Jasmine and explained the situation. I thought he could take a look at her, clean up those scratches and do what is necessary. He asked if her tetanus is up to date. I didn't know.' His jaw clenched as he looked away. He would know…next time. Not that he wanted there to be a next time, but there would be other times…other crises, and he would have the knowledge a father should.

'She's covered.' She kissed her daughter's tear-stained cheek and realised that she herself probably didn't look any better.

'Shall I take her?' Nico offered.

Angel shook her head and held on to her baby. Life would be so much simpler if she could never let go, could keep her safe from the big bad world for ever. She heard people say that the hardest part of parenting was letting go, but it wasn't until now that she knew what that really meant.

With Nico by her side she walked away from Alex, thinking that it felt wrong to be doing so. What was so important that he couldn't come with them? She wanted to tell him he should be with them but didn't—he ought to know.

They reached the bungalow two minutes ahead of the doctor, who arrived apologising for his tardiness, wearing shorts and little else but a reassuring air of calm competence.

As Alex had predicted he cleaned the scratches, applied some antiseptic and managed to distract Jasmine while he gave her a shot of broad-spectrum antibiotic. He advised Angel to keep an eye on the scratches as cats' scratches, he explained, were more prone to infection than dogs', and told her to contact him if she had any concerns at all.

Angel had managed to adopt Alex's what-an-adventure-you've-had tack with Jasmine, who was displaying a youthful resilience that Angel envied. After having a bath and a sandwich or two from the tray that had arrived at the room Jasmine had barely been able to keep her eyes open. She was asleep before her head hit the pillow.

Going back to the living room, Angel persuaded a reluctant Nico that he didn't need to stay.

'Are you sure?'

'Totally. I'm just going to take a shower and head for bed myself.'

Finally alone, she checked on Jasmine before she padded over to the shower, leaving all the interconnecting doors open so that she would hear should Jasmine wake. She didn't, of course, but Angel spent more time stepping out wet to check for some imaginary sound than she did washing off the sand and grime.

Not bothering to dry her hair, she squeezed out the excess water and brushed it back off her face with her fingers. It fell in a heavy rope-like twist down her back. Pulling on the silk robe hung behind the door, she belted it and hurried back to Jasmine's room to double check, her heart suddenly pumping double-time as she stepped into the room.

Angel felt the panic leave her with a soft whoosh. Her daughter hadn't moved since she'd last looked, which was probably all of five minutes ago. It wasn't as if she had expected Jas to have vanished.... Her knees shook a little as she made an effort to gather her composure.

Walking back into the adjoining room, she started on hearing a knock on the door. It wouldn't be Alex—he wouldn't have knocked and maybe he wouldn't even come. Nico would have reported that they were all right. Why should he come?

*Because I want him to!*

*Pull yourself together, Angel. Since when did you need a shoulder to cry on?* Impatient with herself, she went to the door where a smiling maid in the dark blue hotel uniform stood holding a tray.

'The coffee you ordered, miss.'

*Did I?*

Angel thanked the girl and didn't pursue the forgetfulness. Amnesia registered pretty low down in the day's events, so Angel asked the maid to put the tray down on the coffee table.

Two reviving cups later Angel was standing on the veranda when she saw him.

She watched him approach, shading her eyes against the glare of the setting sun that threw pink fingers of light across the silver water. He was too far away for her to make out anything, but his silhouette and his long-legged elegant stride were unmistakable, the way he moved as distinctive as a fingerprint.

Post-caffeine hit she was thinking more clearly, and as she squared her shoulders she knew what he had come to say. Not the words precisely, but definitely the sentiment of the things he would not say in front of Jasmine. And she wasn't going to fight him on it. He was here to blame her, call her a terrible mother and he was right. She had no defence against the truth any more than she had defence left against her feelings for him.

She loved him.

It had taken her long enough to work it out.

When it came to personal relationships she was a blank page. Unlike her, Alex knew about relationships. He'd been in love enough to get married, enough to be devastated when he lost the love of his life, enough to sleep with the first... Well, maybe not the first woman he met but probably the first one who had begged him to take her to bed.

One night of escaping his nightmares, seeking oblivion in mindless sex and who could blame him? It would take a harsh critic to judge him for that but he had clearly judged himself and struggled to wipe the shameful memory from his mind. Marry him.... Yeah, sure, they really were the foundations of a great relationship!

Obviously she knew that Alex was physically attracted to her, and his devotion to Jasmine was not in question. But Angel knew that wasn't enough. Easy thing to say now when she was clear headed, but in his presence—and certainly in his arms—she rarely felt that way.

*Then keep out of his arms, Angel!*

Alex slowed and paused, one hand on the wooden balustrade, coming to a dead halt at the bottom of the shallow flight of wooden steps. The sight of her standing there stole his breath away, the same way she had stolen his heart.

She had every reason to hate him but her generous heart had let him in. She'd given him a second chance, and of course he understood she was wary of trusting him, but if it took him the rest of his life he would convince her.

Her heart started to thud heavily, the echo loud in her ears as he mounted the steps. She could feel the acid taste of self-recrimination in her mouth. He could not possibly blame her more than she did herself.

And she'd lectured him on the responsibilities of being a parent! It was on her watch that this had happened. It didn't matter how many times she went over it in her head, she still couldn't figure out how it had happened; her attention had only been distracted for a moment—and that had been enough.

The blue pedal pushers and white shirt were gone. She now wore a black silk kimono emblazoned with humming birds that ended midcalf to reveal her endless golden legs. His eyes slid hungrily down her body, over the soft, sinuous, sexy curves, and he swallowed, losing his focus as his body surged lustfully. When his gaze settled back on her face her slicked-back hair revealed her face as a perfect oval.

'Is she asleep?'

Angel nodded, lifted her chin and launched into a pre-emptive apology. 'I know it was my fault, totally and—'

He touched a finger to her lips. 'You talk so much rubbish.'

Angel had steeled herself for his accusations; she was totally prepared for his anger. She could have taken that, but what she had no protection from was the incredible tenderness in his face, the concern in his blue eyes and the caressing warmth in his vibrant voice as he took her by the shoulders and looked down into her face, not judging her but offering her support.

'Sorry I was so late but I wanted to be there when the police arrived and explain the situation. And I didn't want to leave until we'd checked the perimeter fence for holes, a classic case of after the horse has bolted, I know, but—' He stopped. 'Here's me babbling and you…you poor baby, you look like hell.'

Her lip quivered. 'I… For God's sake, don't be nice to me, Alex!'

Ignoring her plea, he slid his arms slid around her back. 'Come here.'

Her face crumpled and she stepped into him, feeling his arms close around her as the tears began to flow.

She almost choked on her shame and sense of inadequacy as she struggled to communicate her guilt to him. 'It was all my fault. I—'

'Don't be ridiculous,' he condemned roughly as he passed a hand over her slick wet hair. 'You can't watch a child every second. Even I know that.'

Her teary face lifted. 'I can and I will,' she flashed fiercely, fighting against every instinct she had as she pulled away, dabbing her wet face with her hands and sniffing.

Who'd have thought a sniff could be sexy…? Not Alex, but with Angel there had always been a steep learning curve. Fighting against the temptation to haul her back into his arms, he took a couple deep breaths to conquer and beat the dangerous need into submission. She was shattered physically and emotionally; this was not the time.

'So what did Mark say? You didn't mind me calling him? I just thought it would be less traumatic than a trip to the hospital. I explained about her hip.'

'He was great with her and she's fine. Just superficial scratches and she was very thirsty. He gave her an antibiotic jab to be on the safe side.' Angel's eyes darkened as she shuddered and whispered, 'When I think what could have happened.'

'Don't!'

She closed her mouth over the smart 'easy for you to say' retort, realising with a stab of remorse that it wasn't easy for him. If she still needed it she'd had ample proof today that Alex loved his daughter deeply. Today he had been a rock.

'It is a totally pointless exercise to torture yourself this way.'

She exhaled a long shuddering sigh. 'You're right.'

Some of the gravity left his face as he gave a crooked half smile. 'I am?'

She didn't smile back. 'I don't know how I'll ever thank you for what you did today.'

Alex shook his head, embarrassed by her shining-eyed gratitude. He did not want her gratitude—he wanted her. 'There is nothing to thank me for.'

Her green eyes widened in protest. 'If you hadn't found her before it got dark it could have been hours before she was discovered and anything could have happened.' There were a lot worse things out there than kittens.

He touched her chin, drawing her face round to his as his fingers moved to frame the side of her face. 'You weren't going to do that, remember…?' She nodded, her throat too thick with emotion to speak. 'I was only doing what a dad is meant to and, let's face it,' he added bleakly, 'I have some time to make up for.'

The regret in his voice brought a lump to her throat. No matter what pain it cost her it was worth it for Jasmine to have her father in her life.

'Can I see her?'

Her reply was husked with emotion. 'Of course. You don't have to ask.'

'Since when?'

She gave an uncomfortable half shrug. 'I know I've been defensive and suspicious. It's hard for me to—'

He filled in the blank. *Trust.* And he had played a big part in any trust issues Angel might have.

A strange expression flickered across his face. Taking her totally by surprise, he leaned down and kissed her mouth softly. 'I'll hold you to that promise.'

Balling her hand into a fist to stop it going to her trembling lips, she went with him, but paused at the bedroom door and let him go inside alone.

When he dragged himself away from the sleeping child—it still seemed a total stunning miracle that he had had anything to do with her creation—Alex found Angel outside on the veranda. Night had fallen and the white fairy lights wrapped around the branches in the trees had sparked into life, their glow lending the scene a twinkling other-worldly quality.

'It's a beautiful evening....'

Angel turned and she looked so magnificent that for a moment he couldn't breathe. He stopped midsentence and, loosing a low growl of frustration, he dragged a frustrated hand through his hair.

'This is ridiculous!' His dark brows drew together in a straight, uncompromising line above his hawkish, masterful nose. 'I have so much to say and I'm discussing the weather with you, as if we've just met in the street!'

From where she was standing Angel could feel the waves of emotion rolling off him. She shook her head urgently. 'No, Alex!' She knew what he was going to say—today could only have convinced him more that his duty was to marry her. Everyone thought she was cool and capable and it was an opinion she liked to encourage. Sometimes even she fell for the act, but today had outed her as a spineless, needy wimp who, when the going got tough, fell apart.

'I can't marry you, Alex.'

Aware of how fragile she was, he struggled to control his impatience but he knew it was a battle he was losing.

Pale but composed now, she took a step backwards, widening the gap between them, but not the growing tension. As she continued to hold his gaze she explained the situation in a distant expressionless voice.

'Marriage,' she explained carefully, 'isn't meant to be a penance.'

His eyes darkened with outrage at the suggestion. He started forward and then stopped himself. 'You think marriage to me would be a penance?'

'Oh, God, no!' She took a deep breath and waited for the urgent need to walk into his arms to pass. 'Marriage to you would be…' She stopped, lowered her gaze, thinking, *Too little too late, Angel.*

Way too late. She had been standing there, not wearing her heart on her sleeve, but instead painted like a neon sign across her face!

Still, she mused darkly, she was not telling him anything he didn't already know.

She made herself meet his eyes. 'I know you think it's your duty to marry me.' Feeling the pressure of a future without Alex, a future where she waved goodbye as he drove off with Jasmine for the weekend pressing in on her, heavy and dark, she struggled to maintain eye contact as she told him bluntly. 'I'm not what you need.'

'What I need!' he grated through clenched teeth before swearing in several languages. To hell with this not being the right time, to hell with her being fragile. He had to challenge her blind, wilful stupidity. 'You know nothing, Angel Urquart, but I do. I know that you love me, so why the hell don't you stop putting us both through hell and admit it?'

'Love has got nothing to do with it,' she flared back. 'And don't you dare yell at me. And even if it did…' She shook her head and said firmly, 'There are very good reasons why I can't marry you.'

'Name one,' he challenged, looking unimpressed.

'Well, you don't love me.' Hard words to say without sounding terribly vulnerable and needy but Angel liked to think she pulled it off. 'You don't even like me most of the time….' Taking a moment to flick the damp tail of her hair over one shoulder, she left ample room for him to jump in, but he didn't. He just stood there being unhelpful and looking so gorgeous that she wanted to weep.

'You make me laugh, when you're not making me yell.'

She slung him a reproachful look. Did he have any idea how hard this was for her? 'You think that you should marry me because of Jasmine. I know you mean well…!'

His lips curled in dismissive scorn. 'I am not

some misguided do-gooder!' He took a purposeful step towards her. 'I am a man who wants you, and I intend to have you....'

This outrageously arrogant pronouncement should have made her do many things: laugh scornfully, realise what a lucky escape she'd had, but no. Where on that list of responses came a surge of heavy, hot, toe-curling excitement?

His confidence was total, impregnable. The gleam in his dark eyes as they looked down into her face was hungry.

The urge to melt into him, to lift her face to receive the kiss she could almost taste, was so compelling that resisting it drew a tiny moan from her lips. His silence seemed to be willing her to make that move.

'You know you want me, so why are you fighting it?'

'Yes, I want you.'

The admission upped the tension several more notches. His eyes glowed an incandescent, dizzying blue. The combustible quality that was always there just beneath the surface was no longer buried beneath a veneer of sophistication but right there in her face.

'But you're not talking about wanting, you're talking about marriage. I can't marry you, Alex.'

'I keep hearing that—'

She was unable to retreat any more as the back of her legs had made contact with the small rail that ran around the veranda. She held up her hand, more in hope than any real expectation it would stop his advance, and if he touched her she'd…!

'I can't marry you,' she blurted, 'because I can't have any more children.' His reaction to this information was hard to read because he didn't display any reaction at all.

She had been quiet too when they'd told her the details. She'd thought the overstretched professionals had been relieved when she hadn't broken down, and they had spoken of her healthy attitude.

'Do you understand what I'm saying?'

He tilted his head to one side and surveyed her through narrowed eyes. He didn't buy her supernatural composure for one second. He could feel the pain she was struggling to hide as sharply as if it had been his own. He fought the urge to haul her into his arms and tell her everything was going to be all right. He needed facts.

'How about you tell me what you're saying?'

She responded to the quiet request with a minimal shrug. 'I told you that I needed a Caesarean when Jas was born.' He nodded. 'I might have implied that it was straightforward.'

He hefted out a deep sigh. 'And it wasn't.'

Her shadowed gaze flickered upwards. Remote was the word that came to mind when she tried to read his expression. 'I lost a lot of blood,' she admitted. 'And, well, technical stuff aside, the long and short of it is the chances of me conceiving again are pretty remote.'

He heard her out in silence, his expression growing colder the longer she spoke. 'You could have died—something that slipped your mind, I suppose.'

She was not surprised he was angry. 'Childbirth is very safe these days and my life was never in any real danger. It's not something I think about too often. I have Jasmine, I don't need... It's a closed chapter for me and I didn't see how it could affect us. I mean, how was I to know that you were so ridiculously old-fashioned? I wasn't expecting you to propose.'

'I really don't see… If what you're saying is true…'

Her spine stiffened. 'If!' she ground out tautly. 'Why would I lie?' Did he think she got a kick out of revealing intimate medical details?

'Get down off that high horse, Angel. I'm just trying to make sense of you taking the contraceptive pill unless you were just saying…'

'Oh… I am on the pill, the doctors advised it. Although the chances of me getting pregnant are pretty much the same as winning the lottery, it still is technically possible.' With further tests he had said he could be more precise but Angel, who had had enough of being poked and prodded, had refused.

'Why am I getting the impression that you are giving me only half the story?'

The consultant's final comments came back to her.

'I cannot emphasise how important it would be for you to seek medical advice immediately, *immediately*, Miss Urquart should you even suspect you might be pregnant.'

'If I did by some miracle get pregnant I'd need to be monitored.'

Under his tan Alex paled. 'By that you mean it would be dangerous for you to have a baby... as in life-threateningly dangerous?'

'That,' she said, dodging his gaze, 'is an over-statement. If it did happen—'

'No!'

She gulped at his tone. 'Yes, I know, like I said, the likelihood of it happening is a bit like win-ning the lottery.'

'I mean you will not try.' His hands landed on her shoulders and she could feel the tremors run-ning through him. 'Not now, not ever, will you put your life at risk that way.' It would be just like Angel to pull some stupid stunt like that. 'Do you hear me? Ever!'

Hard not to hear him, not that he was yelling. His voice had dropped to a low bass rumble, the way she'd noticed it did when he was particularly annoyed, but there was nothing wrong with his projection.

His blazing blue eyes burnt into her as he groaned and slid his big hands down her back. She could feel his fingers, warm through the fabric, as they came to rest on her hips, his thumbs on the indent of her waist. 'I've only just found you again. Do you think I'd run the risk of losing you? It would be selfish—Jasmine needs her mother, she needs you.... I need you, Angel. There was a time when I thought about you as my weakness...now I know you are my strength.'

Tears of emotion filled her eyes, spilling like crystal drops down her cheeks. 'You need a woman who can give you everything. You need to wait. I know it might seem impossible now,' she told him gently, 'but one day you'll love someone the way you did Emma. Imagine how awful it would be if, when that time came, you were tied to me. You need love in a marriage, Alex, and you deserve it. And you deserve babies with that person. I've seen you with Jasmine. You'll want a family of your own one day and I can't give it you.'

'You stupid woman.'

She blinked.

'You really are a stupid woman!' The insult was delivered in a voice that held so much love that her eyes filled. 'You already have given me a family—you have given me Jasmine. You and

Jasmine are all the family I want or need, my bolshy, belligerent, beautiful Angelina, my very own Angel. I love you.'

She swallowed and covered the bottom half of her face with her hands. 'But I'm not...'

'You're not second best.'

Her eyes widened at this display of perception. 'I loved Emma,' he agreed quietly. 'And I was glad I was there for her, but we barely had a relationship before I became her carer. We were never really a couple. I think if things had been different we could have been happy but you... you...' He touched her cheek, wonder shining in the incandescent blue of his eyes as he bent to kiss her lips. 'You are my soulmate.'

Joy exploded through her. 'I love you, Alex.'

At the words the tension drained from him and he smiled. Taking her hand, holding her eyes with his, he placed it palm flat against his chest, against the beat of his heart. 'If life took you away from me, it would break. I would break,' he told her in a voice thick and throbbing with the strength of his emotions.

Tears of joy seeping from her eyes, Angel took his hand and kissed the palm lovingly while she looked up at him, vision blurred with tears of joy. 'I won't let you break, Alex,' she promised huskily.

He brushed the tears lovingly away from her face with his thumb. 'Marry me, my Angel.'

'What are you doing tomorrow?'

His grin blazed as he bent his head to claim her lips. 'Becoming the luckiest man on the planet!'

# EPILOGUE

'DADDY!'

It was a title he never tired of hearing. 'Yes, Miss Jasmine?'

'Can we go now?'

'Homework done?'

Jumping up and down impatiently, Jasmine nodded vigorously. 'I've been ready for hours.'

Alex shrugged. 'Don't look at me—so have I. We're waiting for your mother. Blame her.'

'Blame me for what this time?' Angel asked, walking into the room.

'Keeping us waiting,' Jasmine supplied.

'What's the hurry? The snow isn't going to melt anytime soon.' It had been one of the longest winters on record.

'It might! The sun is shining and I want to show Daddy my snowman. He doesn't believe it's taller than him...nearly taller than him.'

'Well, I'm sorry, but getting this one ready is

not a five-minute job.' Angel looked down at the bundle in her arms who was barely visible beneath the layers he was cocooned in. His eyes were closed; his dark lashes lay like a fan across his cheeks. Looking at him it was hard to believe he had kept them awake half the night.

Amazing to think now that when she'd first discovered she was pregnant she had really thought it might split them apart. It was the thing they had both agreed on: no more children. But it had happened anyway, her little miracle, and in the end it had drawn them closer than ever.

She had been more worried about telling Alex than about the pregnancy itself, and she would never forget the look on his face when she had told him. She had never thought to see her big, bold, impossibly brave husband scared, but he had been. She never saw that look again, but she knew the fear was there and the memory of the terror in his eyes would stay with her for ever. Now though, when she thought of it, she was able to see it beside the expression on his face when he had held his newborn son for the first time.

But Alex had been there for her every step of

the way. She didn't think she could have made it through those months with her sanity intact; his wildly overprotective instincts had been in overdrive.

But if ever she became impatient with him when he wrapped her in cotton wool, Angel had reminded herself of that look.

Appearing at her elbow, Alex twitched aside a fold of blue blanket to reveal his son's face. 'His first trip out.'

'Are you sure he'll be warm enough?'

Alex's rich warm laughter rang out. 'In that lot he's more likely to suffer heat exhaustion.'

It still didn't seem real to Alex that he had a son, and, while he loved little Theo more than life itself, the pregnancy itself had been the worst months of his entire life.

The fear of losing Angel had never left him for a single instant. He had felt as though he were walking around with a stone in his chest. He had tried to hide his fears, for Jasmine's sake he had struggled to maintain an illusion at least of a normal family life, but the strain had been immense.

Angel had been amazing. She had sailed through the pregnancy serenely; despite two stays in hospital and intense monitoring she had never once complained.

His wife was truly amazing. He kissed her, a long and lingering kiss that brought a flush to her lovely cheeks.

'What was that for?'

'A man has to take what he can when he can.'

The reminder of the previous afternoon when they had not used the time to catch up with lost sleep but with lost lovemaking brought a deepened flush to her cheeks and a sparkle to her eyes.

'Can I push Theo?' Jasmine asked. 'I'll be very, *very* careful.'

'We'll take turns,' Alex decided as he took control of the pram and zipped up the protective covering, then in a soft aside to his wife added, 'My turn on top later, I think.'

'Marriage is all about give and take.'

And she had married a man who gave a whole lot more than he ever took!

* * * * *

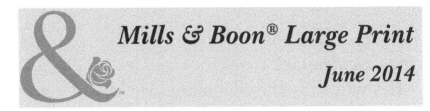

# Mills & Boon® Large Print

## June 2014

0514 Rom LP

# Mills & Boon® Large Print
## July 2014

**A PRIZE BEYOND JEWELS**
Carole Mortimer

**A QUEEN FOR THE TAKING?**
Kate Hewitt

**PRETENDER TO THE THRONE**
Maisey Yates

**AN EXCEPTION TO HIS RULE**
Lindsay Armstrong

**THE SHEIKH'S LAST SEDUCTION**
Jennie Lucas

**ENTHRALLED BY MORETTI**
Cathy Williams

**THE WOMAN SENT TO TAME HIM**
Victoria Parker

**THE PLUS-ONE AGREEMENT**
Charlotte Phillips

**AWAKENED BY HIS TOUCH**
Nikki Logan

**ROAD TRIP WITH THE ELIGIBLE BACHELOR**
Michelle Douglas

**SAFE IN THE TYCOON'S ARMS**
Jennifer Faye

Discover more romance at

# www.millsandboon.co.uk

- ❤ WIN great prizes in our exclusive competitions
- ❤ BUY new titles before they hit the shops
- ❤ BROWSE new books and REVIEW your favourites
- ❤ SAVE on new books with the Mills & Boon® Bookclub™
- ❤ DISCOVER new authors

PLUS, to chat about your favourite reads, get the latest news and find special offers:

- Find us on facebook.com/millsandboon
- Follow us on twitter.com/millsandboonuk
- ❤ Sign up to our newsletter at millsandboon.co.uk